Lily Narcissus

a novel by Jonathan Lerner

For information contact:

Unsolicited Press

Portland, Oregon

www.unsolicitedpress.com

orders@unsolicitedpress.com

619-354-8005

Front Cover Design: 100Covers

Editor: Gage Greenspan

ISBN: 978-1-956692-36-5

for Marcia, Steve, Ashley, David, Higgy, Debbie and Lisa
old China hands

for Lisa

fondly

Jonathan

1.

Lilian Norell first came face to face with Rocky Perreira on one of those days of slow sailing and lazy gossip not far downriver from Taipei. She was passing the tray of sandwiches Hsiu had prepared. They were crustless, fussy for an American picnic, but Hsiu had formerly worked at the Australian consulate and had taken on airs.

Rocky still had his first sailboat then, the one that foundered and sank when he cruised it to the Pescadores— sailed there solo, so he said, which impressed us all enormously. Rocky, Roque Salvador de Freitas Perreira, was the true sailor among us, life spent on the water, life of the party too. But civilized, not salty. Because of Rocky's invitations and urgings and his seductive charm, and because it gave respite from the heat and squalor of Taipei, which was still a poor and grimy place in 1957, boating parties were a frequent diversion for our crowd.

Of course, Lily had met him before. At banquets, at Embassy receptions. But they really took each other in for the first time across that tray of sandwiches. Laid eyes on one another, as it comes back to me now. An almost tactile encounter, though I don't believe they actually touched. I don't think anyone else even noticed. Other than me. People were shielding their eyes from the tropical glare. Everyone was dozily anticipating Lily's tray since spending time on the water makes people hungry—and the circulation of a tray of sandwiches was an unremarkable gesture in that milieu. I was watching, though I realize now that I would have had trouble naming what I saw pass between them. I still have trouble naming it. I probably saw enchantment, but that didn't set off any alarms. Rocky was as fascinating to me as to everyone else.

And we were habituated to enchantment. Nearly everything about Taiwan was strange and marvelous to us. You don't have time to construe subtexts when daily life is a parade of the curious, the grotesque, and the delightful.

Also, I was a child. Well, I was 15.

And I was Lilian's daughter.

So I couldn't have viewed her with clear eyes.

And besides that, I couldn't take my eyes off him.

Everybody loved Rocky. When Lily mentioned him in a letter home to her closest friends, Esther and Rose, she called Rocky "gorgeous". Gorgeous until then was a word she reserved for things like dressy outfits and well-decorated rooms. Or for children, particularly her own and those of her friends. Not for men. Just as "stunning" was a word she mostly used to describe a certain kind of woman, tall and graceful, with hair neatly controlled in a chignon, whether metaphorically or in fact. She wrote to Esther and Rose that Rocky was *simply a gorgeous man. He's our cultural attaché, a confirmed bachelor, his family was originally Portuguese, and he spent some of his childhood in Macau. Looks it too. Very dark, a wonderful smile. I'm dying to get his*

6

story. Honestly, I sometimes feel that we are meeting the League of Nations.

Surely, they had met before that afternoon, but she didn't know him, hadn't had a connection with him yet, when she wrote that. This was early in my father's tour of duty in Formosa. Americans still often called it Formosa then, just as they said Peking then, not Beijing. Ilha Formosa, Beautiful Island, was the name Portuguese venturers gave Taiwan when they encountered it in 1544. It was still beautiful four-plus centuries later when we arrived. Beautiful like a travelogue, like a stage set. Beautiful and unsettling, like a hallucination.

Since this incident occurred early during our time there, it would have been before Rocky's first boat was wrecked. That was a heroic and—now that I think about it—improbable story: Rocky sailing alone, blown by an unpredicted typhoon onto the jagged coast of some obscure islet. One of many unverifiable stories about Rocky, I now understand. But weather prediction was chancy then, so it's not the supposed storm itself that raises doubt. When he returned to Taipei after whatever had actually happened, he took his thousand-watt smile down to that boatyard on the trash-strewn bank of the Tamsui River to haggle over the commission of the missing sloop's identical twin. And soon enough, those deliciously indolent afternoons on the water, orchestrated by maestro Rocky Perreira, resumed.

That day with the sandwiches took place before Lily had made any friends in Taipei. She was worried she might never find any, and she missed her friends at home. She was thrilled and entertained by this exotic new life overseas, mesmerized and intrigued by the foreignness of the city, amused by the social life of the diplomatic community. Was she still nervous that day, handing around the tray? She very quickly became engaged

7

and started enjoying herself. And what a life. She had servants and free time, a car and driver from the motor pool whenever she called for one, luxuries she—we—had never known. But at the time of that particular boating party, she was still looking for some volunteer project to take on, as diplomatic wives were expected to do. And she was sometimes overwhelmed. Rocky's radiant smile and dark eyes must have suddenly felt like safety, a kind of home. I know these things about her now because after half a century her letters to Rose and Esther found their way back to me.

Or, I know some of these things from the letters. From my own recollection, and from what she didn't write, there are other things that I suspect. Maybe I have it wrong. For example, about Rocky feeling like home to her. Maybe Rocky felt more like a holiday.

She was good with words. She wrote often, and Rose and Esther saved those letters in a scrapbook. They thought it would help her treasure the memories when we had resumed our normal life in suburban Washington, after what we all thought at the time was going to be an overseas adventure limited to a single two-year tour of duty. It affects me to read the letters now. They bring my own memories flooding back, along with their shadows and discrepancies, and their sometimes-acute stabs of clarity.

I can picture Rocky's face that day, deeply tan but glowing in the tropical light. He glances for a moment from my mother to me. His lips part in a grin. His teeth are brilliantly white.

Toward the end of her life, frail but always at pains to dress crisply, Lily loved to recount life in Taipei, when she was new to the Orient—as she forever persisted in calling Asia—when everything was still so striking and strange. She elided troubling things, though, and only told the colorful stories, the light ones. The stories of culture-clash comedy and sumptuous pleasure and breathtaking vistas. Of afternoons on the river and picnics packed by a cook whose wealthy family on the Mainland had lost everything when the Communists took over, who arrived penniless in Taipei, found a job in the kitchen of the Australian consul, and there became convinced that "highest class" Westerners would only deign to consume a sandwich if it had been separated from its crusts. Lily acquired her own worldly airs during those years. And in old age, still sipping gin gimlets, the taste for which she first picked up in Taipei, she unspooled her stories. And gave each one this punctuation: "I have always told people, when they ask me what to do with their sons and daughters, 'Get them in the Foreign Service. It's simply a gorgeous life.'"

* * *

Her letters came back to me just last month, hand-delivered by Lewis Eisenstein, Esther's son. All through our childhood, our mothers joked that the two of us would just have to get married so they could be *machetunim*. *Machetunim* is a Yiddish concept that doesn't exist in gentile culture or have an English translation. It means "in-laws of the in-laws." A tribal thing, I guess. The joke was on Esther and Lily, since Lewis turned out to be gay. He was here just now in Hawaii on his honeymoon, as a matter of fact. He and his partner Ken have been together for around thirty years, and Lewis, my age minus three days, is no spring chicken.

9

"I'm starting to feel the tiniest prickle of mortality," Lewis said, with a touch of diffidence, though the diffidence was probably an act.

"Who wouldn't?" I replied.

And, of course, it's finally legal for them to marry. I imagine that hospital visitation rights might have been on their minds, though they both look vigorous enough for seventy-somethings. Lewis was willowy as a kid, but it appears those two have spent a considerable part of their adult lives at the gym. Although they were probably also thinking about financial matters. Esther and Sol got rich, Lewis was an only child and not only inherited but did well for himself anyway, while Ken is an impecunious artist—you get my point.

I don't think I ever saw Lewis again after we went to Taipei in '57. The last clear memory I had of him was of the time the two of us tried to make out. We were bumbling our separate ways through adolescence, possibly taking our mothers' joke seriously. It was awkward and brief and embarrassing, a tiny hint of the possible weirdness on the wedding night of an arranged marriage, or any marriage that concludes a celibate courtship. Now it's clear why Lewis, at least, wouldn't have been comfortable. Why I was so gawky in the moment is murkier, since I'm pretty sure it was initiated by me, and I did like boys. He probably doesn't even remember the incident. It was quite a surprise when he got in touch to tell me he and Ken were coming here to Honolulu, and that he had something of my mother's to give me.

I knew that Rose and Esther had saved Lily's letters. I saw Esther a decade ago, a few years before she died. She mentioned that she had them, and that she was going to give them to me. But she never got around to it. Lewis found them while he was getting rid of her things. Esther told me then that they were all from that first two-year tour in Taipei. We didn't move back to Washington after that, as we were supposed to, and I guess Lily just stopped writing to them. Or at least stopped writing anything they felt like saving.

The letters are yellowed, brittle around the edges, especially the ones typed on onionskin. The letters are attached to the pages of the old scrapbook by strips of cellophane tape, smudged like used Band-Aids. The pages are black construction paper, also crumbling now. The scrapbook's boards are covered in green faux-crocodile skin. It's heavy. I have to prop it up on a table to turn the pages, which tend to drop out of the binding.

After Lewis called, I felt guilty that I didn't immediately invite him and Ken here for a meal or at least a drink. It was as if, from on high, Lily was shooting me a look—Esther too— both of them so house-proud and eager to impart the social graces. They sent us to ballroom dancing lessons too, as teenagers, Lewis and me. That's a skill I have never had occasion to draw upon in later life. I venture to say the same goes for him, though he probably had his disco phase. Our families were so close that we were in and out of each other's houses all the time without formality. But generally, having people over was what was done when I was a child. If the adults met to socialize in bars and restaurants, I never knew it.

But I didn't ask Lewis and Ken over. Lily would have. I don't have people over. I take a gimlet or two myself most evenings, but I drink alone.

Instead, we made a date for lunch at a restaurant. It was surprising how sentimental Lewis was. He gave me an enormous hug when we met. But I don't know the man anymore, so why be surprised? Rather I should be impressed

11

that he showed emotion with such ease. I could probably count on my fingers and toes the times in the last fifty years I'd thought about Lewis Eisenstein, although now that I've been reading Lily's letters, I'm frequently reminded of his family and our childhood milieu. Seeing Lewis again made me realize that for him—for them, the friends we left behind in Bethesda when we made that sideways long jump to Asia in 1957, before jet travel was even a commonplace—we evidently came to occupy a mythic place.

After lunch, in parting, Lewis choked up and told me that as an adult he has always kept a power boat on the Chesapeake—he lives in Annapolis—and his boats, one after the other, have all been named Lady Lily. After my mother. "Her letters," he said, giving me another hug at which I tried not to flinch. It was awkward because I was holding the heavy scrapbook to my chest with both arms. It was also just awkward, period, being hugged by Lewis. I hardly knew him. "The letters, especially the photos she sent. It seemed like you guys were having such a blast, out on the water all the time, on top of everything else you were experiencing. That's what turned me on to boating in the first place. Look."

He took the book and paged through until he found, pasted in among the letters, a once-glossy snapshot. In the foreground, the view is partly blocked by a shoulder and gesturing arm that might have been Rocky's. Must have been Rocky's, that darkly furred forearm and wrist. Beyond, the water is scattered with colorful little sailboats. My brother Jordy, at the tiller of the closest one, is gazing up intently, looking eager. He probably would have been 14, neither quite a boy still nor yet a man. I suppose Rocky was offering him instruction or encouragement. Rocky always offered Jordy encouragement, perhaps too much. Lewis said, "Boating, and her letters—those classy parties, the limousines, I ate it all right up." Lady Lily. I wonder how Esther felt about that, especially after Lily disappeared from her life.

"Lewis," I said, "there weren't limousines. The cars from the motor pool were, I don't know, Ford sedans."

He and Ken were staying at Waikiki and invited me to go outrigger-canoe surfing with them. They're into adventure travel; they were heading on to the Big Island the next week to hike Volcanoes National Park, since Kīlauea had simmered down and people could get in again. But I begged off. I've had enough adventures traveling. And I may just be done with boats, too.

* * *

Edgewater Hotel, Waikiki
September 23, 1957
Dearest Girls,

Aloha from paradise! We arrived in Honolulu yesterday, after five days crossing the magnificent Pacific from San Francisco aboard the S.S. Lurline. *The ship was a dream. The most lush, plush existence, the décor was all beautiful contemporary like you and I adore. I thought of you two constantly.*

My most strenuous activity was a daily hula class. You should have seen some of the grandmas trying to keep up, which made me feel quite glamorous. I shall practice it every day so that I can demonstrate when I come home. There were endless activities to *keep the kids occupied, including a ping-pong tournament, which I am proud to inform you was won by my darling daughter. Of course, the children also picked up a few bad habits on the ship, such as gambling—they do a game of horse racing, like a board game with dice, only played on a course laid out all the way across the ballroom floor, and a steward moves these big wooden horses along. There was also a ship's pool—everybody makes a wager on the distance traveled since the day before. Jordy had the thrill of winning $54 from that. We celebrated the kids' victories by drinking the bottle of champagne you two thoughtfully sent, which was awaiting us in our cabin when we came aboard. Very good it was too. So in addition to gambling, the children are developing a taste for alcohol. As a matter of fact, and unbeknownst to us, young Master Norell chose to spend some of his winnings in the cocktail lounge! He might look old for thirteen, but we were shocked. Sid raised a stink with the purser, you can imagine. And as for what went on between him and Jordy, don't ask.*

* * *

I quite clearly remember seeing her write this first letter, during that stopover in Hawaii. We were staying in a shady cottage in a grove of palms on the hotel grounds. My father, brother, and I came up from the beach to find Lily sitting out on the lanai. On the table before her was a platter of cut fruit: some pineapple, but mostly fruit we had never seen, papaya and guava, mango and starfruit, all glistening orange and gold. The gentle air on my bare shoulders, where droplets of saltwater were evaporating, the hypnotic boom of the surf, the rattling palm fronds, bougainvillea in drapes of magenta and coral,

14

heavy purplish banana flowers tumescent to the point of bursting—I suppose this moment remains so vivid because it was my first sensory immersion in the tropics. A postcard image in Kodachrome. Now of course I've spent most of a lifetime in tropical places: on islands, at beaches, in remote jungle locations. Not all of those places were postcard-pretty.

Next to the platter of fruit was a bottle of nail polish and Lily's portable typewriter. That was a sleek little Olivetti Lettera 22. She had swooned over one like it, which she saw on display as an example of avant-garde industrial design at the Museum of Modern Art when she and Esther and Rose took a wives-only weekend in New York. Lily always loved whatever was the latest; the museum's validation of the typewriter as an art object must have made it irresistible. Her friends surprised her with this one as a going-away present. It was aqua in color—like the Chevy convertibles of that year, like the sea at Waikiki—with a zippered vinyl carrying case to match. "Did you kids have fun?" Lily asked brightly. "I'm writing to the girls." She waved her newly lacquered fingertips, a single gesture both to dry them and to indicate the tray. Ever-efficient Lily. "Try some of this divine fruit and give me fifteen more minutes. Then, Lauren, I'll do your nails."

Maybe it was our interruption that caused her to omit a few other examples of the joys of shipboard travel from that letter. I had forgotten about winning the ping-pong tournament. I clearly remember, though, that Lily entered me in the Miss Lurline contest, a beauty pageant, another way for passengers to stay amused. I never would have thought to enter myself. You had to be at least 16, which I was not yet, but my mother blithely put me forward anyway and told me to lie— well, the word she used was "fib"—if anybody asked. The only

15

bit I remember with clarity is the talent portion. I simply announced that I had beat everybody at ping-pong the day before. I knew this was subversive, but I hated faking my age even if it was only a sin of omission, and saying this ensured I would lose, which got me out of posing for the ship's photographer while wearing a ribbon and cardboard crown. I would have preferred choosing my own outfits and filing my nails without painting them.

Then there was Jordy's further escapade. We were at breakfast in the dining room, table for four, the morning after he spent his winnings in the bar. "I'm disappointed in you, son," said Sid.

Jordy picked up the cup at his place and held it out toward a waiter who was pouring coffee at the next table.

"You're too young to drink coffee. And don't ignore me." Sid hadn't exactly raised his voice, but his tone was commanding. The woman at the next table looked in our direction. Then her husband did too.

"Do you want me to get you an aspirin, honey?" Lily asked Jordy, managing an ambiguous smile that was at once maternally solicitous toward him while artfully carefree in the direction of the neighbors.

"Old enough to enjoy this trip at liberty, I thought—but no. Let's say you're confined to quarters today." Sid had been in the navy during the war, though he'd only had a desk job in Washington—something to do with information. I never knew much about it. He seemed to be using this sea voyage, and that anachronistic naval jargon, as a way to bolster his bona fides. While the three of us allowed ourselves to be diverted by the ship's luxuries and entertainments, he spent most of the crossing in the library, reading naval histories and Captain Horatio Hornblower novels, or else chatting up the ship's officers over cocktails. *We saw so little of him,* Lily wrote, *that I was about to have him declared man overboard.*

Jordy sipped from his coffee and did that thing of his, letting his face shift from neutral into a half-smile. This bit of artifice might convey to an observer that he was a slow-witted, which he wasn't, or that he was carefully pondering what he'd just heard, which he sometimes did. But his gradual half-smile could as easily have been a form of protection to fend something off. In this case it more likely was an expression of rebellion, contempt for what our father was saying. He was in the throes of puberty around the time we went to Taipei. His voice had become scratchy. You could almost watch his face changing, as if he were molting, growing too big to be contained in a tender boy's skin. He had been a cute, soft kid. Now his jawline was defining itself, his face lengthening.

Lily and Sid were berthed in a double. I was sharing with a girl who was on her way to Honolulu to join her husband, a lieutenant at Pearl Harbor. Jordy, strangely, had a cabin by himself. Sid instructed him to stay there until he was called. It was an inside cabin without a porthole. To my little brother, who could be bratty and impatient, but who was probably suffering from hormonal changes, this probably felt like a life sentence in solitary. So he made a break for it. When we couldn't find him, Lily began to panic and insisted on reporting his disappearance. Sid, as tightly contained as a pressure cooker, did the talking. A search was organized, with uniformed crew members at pains to make the effort appear as if it weren't happening so as not to alarm other passengers.

I figured they'd find him crouched in a lifeboat. Actually, he had slipped through one of those nearly imperceptible portals to the part of the ship passengers were never supposed to see. He was discovered helping a Filipina laundress fold sheets. Surely his presence made her uncomfortable, but she probably didn't feel in a position to challenge him for being there. If she had, I don't know for a fact that he would have said, "My father is in the Foreign Service so I am allowed to do anything I want," but that is the sort of line, or attitude anyway, Jordy often resorted to when in a jam later in life—when he so often found himself in a jam.

* * *

Lily, Esther, and Rose often sat around the Formica tables in one another's kitchen, downing quantities of weakly percolated coffee and genially kvetching. It was a form of shared bonding, or release, like the consciousness-raising groups that came along with the emergence of the women's movement a few years later—I attended one or two of those, when I was back in the States for college. Except theirs lacked the consciousness-raising aspect. They were happy to discuss us kids as irritants, but they fully expected every one of us to excel in life. And some of us did, or did well enough. But the exasperated-mom routines were a hedge against our possible failures being construed as their fault.

As the oldest of all their children, and a girl, they assumed I was a future member of such a sisterhood or, rather, matronhood. They liked when I sat with them—sometimes. Sometimes the conversation turned to their husbands, or to other people's marriages. Sometimes it grew hushed because someone had been diagnosed with the great unmentionable, cancer, or the great euphemism, female trouble, meaning an unwanted pregnancy and perhaps an abortion. At those moments, the hushed moments, I understood that I wasn't supposed to stick around. I was only permitted to hear the standard-issue motherly complaints.

"Vey iz mir," I remember Esther whining one time. "*Now* Lewis wants me to schlep him to Georgetown for *art history* classes. There's this fellow who takes kids to the National Gallery and God knows where to discuss what? Those pictures of *naked men falling from the sky?*" Lewis retired last year as managing partner of the Washington office of an international architecture firm: not a failure. My own checkered career path, my personal life too, would have been harder or maybe impossible for them to approve in advance. Though its aspects of sacrifice and high-mindedness eventually won their admiration.

But I can think of several reasons why, when composing that first letter home, Lily didn't put in Jordy's vanishing act aboard the *Lurline*. Maybe it was as simple as our interrupting her that day at the Olivetti. Or maybe it was because she couldn't ignore the fact that she was, at that moment, nearly halfway around the world, far out on an island in the middle of a shimmering sea, headed into a blurry unknown. Something else was troubling her, which she had a stronger need to tell the girls.

I guess two years in Formosa will take care of this life of ease. I'm bracing for the worst. We have one more day here in Hawaii. The rest of the family is terribly excited, and for all their sakes I'm trying not to show it, but I am filled with trepidation. I keep thinking about all those trips we had to make downtown to the State Department clinic for shots—typhoid, typhus, cholera, yellow fever—and what about the diseases they don't have vaccines for like malaria and God forbid leprosy? I already miss Bethesda and normal life and you two and everybody, very much.

So, sinking into the western sky, I remain your very own

Lily

* * *

After reading that letter, I went looking for the Edgewater Hotel. I had hardly been to Waikiki since I retired to Honolulu nearly a decade ago. Naturally, it had changed in all the years since 1957. Not naturally as in the forces of nature, but from the inexorable nature of development in general, and a tourism economy in particular. At Waikiki Beach, there were no more of those laid-back, low-rise resorts with bungalows scattered under the palms. There was no more Edgewater Hotel at all. One or another massive tower stippled with balconies has taken its spot. I could easily research which, but they're interchangeable and they were not what I was looking for. I walked through the lobby of one, out to its terrace overlooking the surf, and ordered an iced coffee. At the table next to mine, a mother and a sulky teenage girl were enacting the brittle cheeriness of family travel.

We flew out from Honolulu to Tokyo at midnight on Japan Airlines. "Isn't this simply charming?" Lily said about the hot towels handed out by the stewardesses before take-off, and said again when that was repeated at several points in the journey; it's not uncommon now, but at the time, this was an amenity and an expression of Japanese culture we had never encountered. The plane was a DC-7, I think. Jordy would know, obsessed for life with aircraft as our journey halfway around the world to Taipei had rendered him. But, of course, I can't ask Jordy now. I do know that the plane had four loudly thrumming propeller engines, and that the flight took forever.

We crossed the International Date Line and landed for refueling on Wake Island. There, in the dark, at some unknown hour in some indeterminate time zone, we disembarked for a breakfast that was served at long tables in a Quonset hut left over from the war. Back on the plane, still flying through the dark, we were served another breakfast. And when we had landed in Japan and transferred to a hotel—just for the day, so we could shower and change, since we were flying on to Taipei that same night—but now, at 8 a.m. local time, there was another breakfast still. "Oy," Lily said several times, "I'm a bissel dismentaled." It was her Aunt Minna's malapropism, something Lily would say back then to make fun of herself. Though not too many months after that, she wouldn't have done that anymore. Made fun of herself, I mean.

Already disoriented by that long, time-zone-scrambling crossing, we experienced our bewilderingly alien first twelve hours of Asia. From the Tokyo airport that night while waiting for our repeatedly delayed onward flight, Lily penned a letter to Rose and Esther. Of the letters I have, it's the only one not typed. I suppose the Olivetti was in our checked luggage. She wrote it on a flimsy blue aerogramme with one of the leaky ballpoint pens of the day. It's wobbly and blotched, but legible. Lily had exquisite penmanship.

There are skyscrapers going up, but we passed neighborhoods that are still flattened, rubble from the bombings. The people wear everything from the traditional kimonos to the 1927 flapper era of tight, short skirts and knickers on the men, to some modern styles, with plenty of people in dirty, torn rags. We walked on the Ginza, which is like their Broadway, and is extremely congested. It was a strange feeling for us to be the foreigners, since we only saw a handful of non-Oriental faces all day. We had lots of laughs with the language and the money—360 yen equals $1, so it's easy to pretend to be rich. We took a cab and Sid couldn't understand how much the driver wanted so he gave him 500 yen—turned out it should have been 80—good for international relations. Lauren's turquoise ballet flats caused many stares and giggles. Anyway, I couldn't help remembering the Japanese prison camps and death marches, altho everyone was extremely polite and friendly and bowed to the ground.

But I've been a nervous wreck all day. Now we're about to board a flight on Civil Air Transport, an airline I'd never heard of. They're headquartered in Taipei—should this make me more or less confident? Anyhoo, tomorrow nite we will lay our heads down there for 2 yrs. Bulletin, or cry for help, will be forthcoming shortly—but if there is a big silence, you'll know I had a complete breakdown at the sight of it. My next communication may be a message in a bottle.

Love,
Lily

P. S. We just learned that Marian Anderson is on our flight—performing in Taipei this week. So the place does have some culture, after all. Sid and I attended her concert at the Lincoln Memorial in '39, when the D.A.R. wouldn't let her sing at Constitution Hall since she's a Negro. We weren't even married yet. The strangest thing—of course I've never met Miss Anderson in person, but it suddenly feels as if we have an old friend traveling with us.

* * *

I had no idea then that she was frightened—she always presented herself as so perfectly composed. As for Sid, if he was nervous, he wouldn't have admitted it to himself, let alone put it in writing. Anyway, for Jordy and me all this was pure adventure. Jordy loved those long flights. He would get himself invited into the cockpit. You could do that back then, kids especially. The stewardess gave out little junior-pilot pins, too. He would spend as much time up front as the pilots would give him, barraging them with questions and hanging onto their stories. I was just entranced by how different everything was, how much difference there was, and how it kept coming at us. Entranced by the big wide world, you might say. Social studies and geography had been my favorite subjects in school. Now social studies and geography were materializing all around me, so kaleidoscopically that all I could do was try taking everything in. I'm not the least perceptive person in the world, but just then when our life was changing so fast, I hardly bothered to notice what my mother might have been feeling.

Surely Marian Anderson, the celebrity, would have been the first to disembark when that Civil Air Transport DC-6 rumbled to a halt at the airport terminal in Taipei. It must be a trick of memory that I see myself standing shoulder to shoulder with my parents and brother in the aircraft's open doorway as the steps were wheeled into place. I recall being dazzled, nearly blinded, by the sun after the all-night flight, and gasping at the hot inrush of air with its whiffs of aviation fuel and tropical rot.

Two American couples stood below, waiting to greet us. The first of so many reception lines. Dyson van Kirk, Sid's boss at ICA—the foreign aid unit of the State Department where he would be working—was accompanied by his wife, Barbara. They greeted us with restrained, or perhaps ambivalent, heartiness. I remember her handshake as particularly limp, but I was feeling suddenly limp myself. Alongside them stood another couple, Henry and Ella Mitnick. Ella's hair stuck out, dark and thick. "I'm the Welcoming Committee!" she said, approaching Lily with a hectic lurch. "Usually it wouldn't be just me, of course! But all the other members have either gone on home leave or gotten themselves involved in some other project. I've had to beat the bushes for a couple of new members. I'd ask you, but you'd have to have been here for a while and—wait til you're settled."

Ambiguity or inscrutability or even limp boredom were probably closer to what Lily was expecting to be met with as she stepped foot onto the terra firma of Taiwan. As the flight came to an end, she had carefully fixed her face, smoothed her blouse, girded for the unknown. Now, under Ella's advance, her smile stiffened. "We are all just so excited to finally be here," Lily said calmly, turning her attention from Ella back to Mrs. van Kirk, and repeating, "So excited. The kids are practically beside themselves." Although, in truth, Jordy and I were just dazed. Barbara van Kirk smiled faintly, or with resignation. Dyson van

Kirk was already engaged with Sid, having said his perfunctory hellos to the rest of us, who, being the dependents, were of no interest to him. Henry Mitnick made the least impression of all that day. He must have been brought along so Ella didn't have to come alone. And because the diplomatic community was overwhelmingly comprised of married couples, accompanying her was just the thing to do. That must have made Rocky stand out when Lily encountered him—Rocky being single in such a coupled-up world.

Rocky being single, plus his many other charms.

* * *

At first, Lily's letters were like travelogues. Everything was so vivid and different, and there was so much to describe. She would use carbon paper to make three copies of each as she typed. These she would send to different people back home to pass around. But for the one going to Esther and Rose, she would often roll the original back into the carriage of the aqua Olivetti and add a postscript.

Taipei
October 6, 1957
Dear Friends, one and all,

We have been here for one week, and I hardly know how to tell you about our new life. But here goes.

We arrived very early last Sunday morning. We were in the plane all night from Tokyo, stopping at Okinawa to refuel, which just made the trip feel interminable. I must admit that it was with some fear and trembling that I climbed back on board to face the last leg of our journey and the unknown quantity of Formosa. We were met at the airport by Sid's boss and his wife, along with the Welcoming Committee—consisting of one Ella Mitnick. Imagine my surprise! We were then taken to our house, and we were all most delighted. Many of the Americans who are here with Sid's agency live in houses like ours that were built by the Japanese when they occupied Formosa before the war. Although it is what's called "Western style" and might not look out of place in Florida, it still has a bit of a Japanese feel, which I adore. Every house has a high wall around it, which takes some getting used to, but when you are inside (you get in by ringing a bell and your servant admits you) it is very pleasant to have a walled garden à la Georgetown.

But the best part was our greeting by our two smiling servants—we have a male cook and an amah, and they are sensational. They came highly recommended and have worked for other diplomatic families, so I do not need to tell them anything about the boiling of the water or which local vegetables we may or may not eat—which is good because I can't keep all that straight myself. Hsiu is a slender, very nice-looking young man of 28. He plans, cooks, and serves all the meals, and is generally in charge of the household. Wei is adorable—short and plump—she's older, but I can't tell by how much. She cleans and does the laundry daily. Such a laundress—our clothes could all be on exhibition in a department store window. They both speak some English, but Hsiu and I often have long, animated discussions about such things as whether it is better to buy eggs in the local market or at the U.S. Commissary—and he definitely tells me that it is cheaper and better in one of those places, but the trouble is that I cannot get it clear which one.

Also, I am afraid I have lost face with Hsiu a little as of today. I asked him when he would cook us some Chinese food and he explained that he could not until we had some rice bowls and chopsticks and other dishes necessary to serve them. So, I went shopping at the nearby street market and purchased said items. However, he was rather disgusted with me since I had bought what I considered attractive blue and green pottery bowls, and he informed me that he would never eat out of pottery bowls like that—they are for country people and I should have bought china ones. He is from the Mainland and is supposed to have come from a wealthy family.

Well, surely you have gotten the faint impression that we are living in a very elegant style. But then there is the rest of the city outside of our high walls. It is like suddenly being placed back in time. Most of the people are living and working just as they did centuries ago. The city is dusty, mostly dirty, teeming with busy humanity, pedicabs, bicycles, people pushing carts or pulling carts, water buffalo pulling carts, chickens, goats, turkeys, children, and more children. Many people live in tiny shacks—there is a warren of these, erected and occupied by squatters on the empty ground right at the end of our lane, which is incidentally unpaved and has open ditches filled with sewage called "benjos" running along both sides. People also live in the back or front of their little stores and businesses. The families' daily routines happen in public. You can see them bathing or eating or washing clothes or the children going to the toilet.

Once you have gotten over the first shock of life as you have never seen it before, a ride down the street is better than a show. And even though many are poor, there are no beggars, and all the children look happy. The babies always have someone to hold them, from very ancient grandpas or grandmas to brothers or sisters who are barely big enough to walk themselves. The traffic is wild and there seem to be no rules, except every man for himself. There are potholes and puddles everywhere.

Our car won't arrive for another month, as it is coming by sea along with our household effects. I am hoping that by then I will be able to face taking the wheel, but at the moment I prefer to be a passenger. We have been driven a little way outside of the city, and the countryside is absolutely beautiful—very rich and lush. In the background are gorgeous mountains terraced for rice paddies, everything deliciously green.

Sid and I have already met many of the people from his agency. They are simply charming and friendly. We were invited to three dinner parties last week, and tonight there will be a large official cocktail party to introduce us formally to all the people he works with. The children seem to be fitting in well at the International School, too.

Well, I have exhausted myself with this long letter. Anyway, Sid will be home from the office shortly, and I must figure out something smashing to wear to this affair since it's in our honor. Really, you can see that we are having a fascinating time so far. I only wish you all could be here with us.

Love to all friends and relations,
Lily

* * *

In a postscript to Rose and Esther, Lily mostly disparaged Ella Mitnick. *I thought it was a stroke of luck meeting a Jewish family right away. But she is definitely not my cup of tea. I innocently asked if there are any Jewish activities for the kids, and she practically yelled at me, "Norell? You're not Jewish? Is that an Ellis Island name? I took you for a* shiksa*!" And then proceeded to tell me about this one and that one—people whom I hadn't even met— mostly relating her personal commentary on, ahem, "the* goyim *we're surrounded by," and what she thinks they think of us. I would prefer to draw my own conclusions if you don't mind.* Not *what I would call a highly skilled diplomat.*

It's curious, her reaction to Ella, whom I recall as being little different in comportment from Rose or Esther or any of the women in my parents' circle back home. It could have been a sign that Lily was casting off, drifting from that world she'd known—a sign written on water. She grudgingly dismissed Henry, Ella's husband and a Harvard economist, as *a nebbish, but a brain.*

She had written that she was afraid. But from the first, Lily mainly portrayed herself as confident and fascinated. When I read her letters now, my mind immediately goes to an image of her dressing to go out. She put a lot into it and doing so served her well. There is a postscript to another letter, addressed to Esther, written not long after we arrived: *I am so relieved to find that my wardrobe is perfectly adequate. Outfits that are two and three years old are just stunning here.*

A few weeks after our arrival, there was a parade on the anniversary of the founding of the Republic of China. October 10, or Double Ten Day. *We watched it from the roof of Sid's building downtown and were right opposite the stands in which were seated the Generalissimo and Madame Chiang Kai-shek! He looked rather forbidding—and people say she is made of cast iron, but they both looked poised and gracious. That evening we went to a cocktail party at the Foreign Minister's residence, which was magnificent—outdoor garden with stone pagodas and bridges over streams, colored lanterns and hundreds of people, Chinese women in elegant brocade dresses with high collars and fancy frog closures.* Lily always appreciated a beautiful costume.

There was a tea held in honor of recently arrived diplomatic wives. It was put on by the wife of the American ambassador, *a real character complete with a wig and a mesh snood. They live outside the city up on Grass Mountain, where there are gorgeous views and hot springs baths. We were all invited to take a dip right then. Can you imagine?*

Confidence—even the projection of false confidence, if that what she was putting forth—was more elusive for Jordy and me. We were enrolled at the International School a day after arriving in Taipei, although the school year had started a month before. High school is high school everywhere—You don't want to be a new kid joining the class late. Maybe Lily was reassured by her wardrobe, but I remember that mortifying first day and my once-over from all the girls—it seemed that ballet flats were out, or hadn't yet arrived. And to my distress, saddle shoes—of which I had none—were still in. My once-over from the boys was not about clothes. This was a gantlet, if only a psychological one. Jordy's brief career at that school was mainly notable for the trouble he got into. Trouble at that school, and at every one he attended after that.

* * *

I certainly didn't understand Jordy then. I'm not sure I understand him now. And I don't know that Lily and Sid ever really tried.

As a kid, he was bursting with intensity. Neither he nor I had ever flown before that trip to Taipei, when he caught airplane fever. He was seduced by mechanical structures, what held things together and made them work. Even low-tech things. In the streets of Taipei, he was captivated by the carts pulled by water buffalo with their hand-hewn wooden wheels that were six feet in diameter. He was even interested in the cruder ones pushed or pulled by sweating coolies, contraptions cobbled together from discarded crates and old baby-carriage wheels or bicycle wheels or wheels salvaged from junked cars. Maybe because their simplicity was so visible, or because of their ostensible simplicity, it seemed that anybody could construct one.

He was enchanted, too, by the birdcages made of toothpick-thin bamboo slats, which were for sale in the street markets. He couldn't get over their transparent lightness and paradoxical strength, and was especially taken with the fanciest cages that mimicked temples in form, complete with curved roof ridges and upturned corners. He liked their architectural mimicry but loved their revealed complexity.

Jordy loved the temples of Taipei for the same reasons. Everyone else—other Westerners like us, I mean—would be enraptured by the ornament and symbolism and gaudiness. The high-relief ceramic friezes set along the cornices, brightly glazed polychrome narratives of dragons and elephants and battles, emperors and courtiers in splendid raiment and ladies tripping over arched bridges. The carving and filigree, the fretworked wooden shutters, the elegant colonnades of slim, round, red-lacquered posts supporting slim, round, red-lacquered beams. But Jordy was instead fascinated by how those shutters could be folded back so that whole walls could be opened onto shadowy, incense-veiled sanctums. He was dumbfounded by the posts and beams. Not for their lustrous lacquer but for how they were morticed together and, delicacy notwithstanding, contrived to hold up all those stone balustrades and ceramic friezes and the heavy earthenware barrel tile that paved the roofs.

It was a similar complexity that first entranced him about airplanes, the enigma of heavier-than-air flight. He badgered the pilots for their stories. But he was as interested in their explanations of the physics and mechanics of flying as in their tales of air battles during the war. I don't think the glittery arrays of gauges and switches in the cockpit did that much for him; he was more curious about the information those gadgets conveyed, the processes they controlled.

It was on that long flight from Honolulu to Tokyo that he returned to his seat next to mine bubbling over about ailerons and flaps and how they kept a plane aloft, or whatever it is they do. I couldn't shut him up. When we lived in Taipei, Jordy spent hours piecing together model planes. He went to the PX every week to buy another model kit. They were plastic and had pieces that were so tiny he had to handle them with tweezers while he glued them into place with Testors cement. I can smell the stuff just picturing it, acrid but provocative. Jordy's room always smelled of it. It probably affected his brain. His first addiction, I guess. Model airplane glue. First addiction to a substance, I mean. He was already hooked on planes.

It's odd. This absorption, this passion of his. Considering that he never got excited about much in school. He could have been a mathematician or an engineer or an architect with a little encouragement or some decent teaching. When we were little, Lily used to tell us that we could grow up to be anything, that it was the great thing about our country. I could be a

Congresswoman—there were one or two of them back then—
or even a doctor. As a matter of fact, our pediatrician was a
woman, so that career didn't seem particularly outlandish.
When Lily realized that Jordy loved complicated constructions
and machines that flew, in addition to telling him he could be
the first Jewish president of the United States, she sometimes
mentioned careers like aeronautical engineering. The Russians
sent up Sputnik in 1957, within a few days of our arrival in
Taipei, and all the talk—in panicked tones—was suddenly
about satellites and spaceships. "You could go to Mars," Lily
actually said to Jordy once. As it happened, his interest in the
engineering aspects was finally eclipsed by his passion for flying
itself. He never lost his craving to defy gravity and leave this
earth.

* * *

*The latest chapter in our Oriental saga: we have been having
our house painted. A crew of about twelve men arrives every
morning at eight and start in—it's been a problem to get into the
bathroom because, if there wasn't already one painting in there, I'd
find one on a ladder outside looking in. And of course, I can't
converse with them except for the universal "Okay." which every
single Chinese apparently knows. In order to show them that I think
they are doing fine work, I periodically go up to the foreman and
say "Okay," and he beams and says "Okay" to me, and everything
is okay. However, we did run into quite a to-do when I decided to
have the crown moldings painted the same shade as the walls—my
cook, Hsiu, acted as the interpreter. I only understand every tenth
word that Hsiu says, and he and the paint foreman speak different*

dialects, so it was all very merry and gay and they both acted as if I were a little crazy. The foreman finally issued some loud instructions, but I could see that it was against his better judgment. In addition to the paint crew, we have had a man cleaning floors right behind them, a man cleaning windows, a man making new screens, and the gardener trimming bushes. And then when the drapery man arrived, I retired next door to my neighbor Gladys Walter's and had a drink with her.

Ah—the drapery man—honestly, you won't believe it—I guess you think I am exaggerating but every little thing is so funny and different. Well, my drapery man first brought all his samples to show me tied up in a little cloth on the front of his bicycle. Then, after he had hung the living room draperies, I complained that some were longer than others. He said he would take care of it, and so the next day (in the midst of the painters) he arrived on his bicycle, behind which he was pulling a little cart, and on the cart reposed a seamstress and a peddle sewing machine. Is that service or not?

* * *

But Lily's letters are disconcerting me. My memories of Taiwan had flattened and collapsed onto each other, a pile of snapshots, static images. It'd been a long time since I really thought about Taiwan, except in the most fragmented way, in unconnected glimpses. Rice-paddies spilling down a mountainside, cascades of blindingly supersaturated green. The corpse of a dog in the street, alive with flies. The guy who set up his table in our lane and fashioned elaborate figurines from tinted dough—opera characters in full makeup and costume, soldiers, tigers and dragons—to sell to children for pennies. A man with a horrifying goiter like an eggplant drooping from his neck. These images are beautiful and awful, provoking sensations within me. The revolting stench of "stinky tofu" from the street vendor's wok. The bumpy pedicab ride on the unpaved lanes while heading to my friend Rosemary's house. The shriek and twang of the outdoor opera.

They're random, these images, like floaters when you close your eyes—not like Lily's letters, with their sharp pictures and clear chronology. She deals out anecdotes separately—complete little narratives. But why should I find my own recollections in my mother's correspondence? I kept a diary back then. Didn't every teenage girl do that? Do they still? Surely not, their memories are stored on their phones as selfies. Why use words, kids—but don't get me started. My diary was a little, red faux-leather book with a strap closure and tiny brass lock. Jordy was constantly trying to find the key to expose his big sister's inner life. Whatever that inner life may have amounted to. Maybe I described it in those pages. But I doubt it, and that little book is long lost.

* * *

I expected to feel low when we arrived, but I can honestly say that I've loved every minute so far. The people, for the most part, are interesting and delightful. Everyone seems to have such an unusual life story that I sometimes feel we must be quite boring to them. I have been especially lucky with my neighbors. We have the middle one in a row of five identical houses on our side of the lane, all occupied by colleagues of Sid's, with gardens separated by common walls. Right next door are the Billy Walters. He is the legal advisor for the ICA mission and has a real dry sense of humor. Gladys, his wife, must be the most well-loved person in the diplomatic community. Unlike the other wives, she does not go in for charitable projects as such. She only tries to make everyone happy. They're from Alabama and have lived overseas for years and years—in Korea for six years, where they were evacuated at the beginning of the war, and then spent another five in Indonesia. They have one little boy who was adopted and is half-Indonesian and half-Western. It seems that Gladys had lost a baby, and the next day this infant was abandoned on the Embassy doorstep. They felt it was an act of God and immediately adopted him. Isn't that one for Ripley's Believe It or Not!? *You guys would love her. She had a dinner party for us—it was hilarious—she had different hats for everyone and pasted long false eyelashes on me. And there were all sorts of games—she made up a kitchen orchestra with utensils.*

It sounds silly, but it was the first party here I thoroughly enjoyed. I didn't feel so scrutinized. This place can feel very much like a small town, and I don't yet know who whispers to whom. If you know what I mean.

* * *

I saw Gladys Walter once years later when I passed through Washington. It would have been in the early Seventies. The Walters had retired and were living in Georgetown. Eric—the abandoned infant they adopted in Jakarta—was following in Billy's footsteps by working on his Master's in International Relations at Hopkins and was headed for the Foreign Service himself. Gladys was as warm as ever. She was still drinking in the middle of the day, but only white wine spritzers, which she dismissed with a wave as "poor folks' champagne." She still loved a party, and when I called to ask if I could visit, she wanted to use it as an excuse to throw a luncheon for a group of Old China Hands—the informal club of people who'd served in Taiwan or on the Mainland before the Nationalists abandoned it to Mao and Company. She said, "I can order in from the Peking. We'll have chopsticks and rice wine!" I fended that off, protesting that I could hardly remember any of the people she might invite. That wasn't exactly true, and they would all at least know who I was. I was Lily's daughter, and Lily went on to become rather well-known within that world.

I just wanted to see Gladys. She'd been such a presence when we were first in Taipei, being right there over the wall. We were always popping in and out of each other's houses. Not literally, I guess, because the wall was six feet high and you had to go out into the lane and then ring to get back in through the gate next door. Although, there was the time she organized a progressive party involving three or four adjacent households. She had step ladders placed against the walls so the guests could climb up and over between each stop, the level of peril increasing as the gin flowed and the hour grew late. When guests descended the ladder into her garden, Gladys sprayed them with a hose. Everybody thought it was hilarious. "That Gladys. Such a scream." I remembered her as oddly steadying, despite the screwball persona. She was a sort of mentor to Lily, having already been in Asia with State for such a long time. She'd seen it all and figured out a way to participate while remaining detached. Perhaps I should say, while remaining anesthetized. She welcomed me that toasty October afternoon in Georgetown as fondly as ever. We sat out on her terrace—another enclosed garden, but hardly mistakable for being in the tropics, with its English ivy rusting against brick walls and a dwarf maple dripping bronze.

"Oh, I'm so glad to hear about your brother," Gladys said. At the time, Jordy was flying for Air America, which was based in Thailand. He was one of their youngest pilots. "I know he's given your mother and father plenty of worry—you hear things—the grapevine—but it sounds like he's settling down now and found something he loves doing. Well, we're all worried about the boys in the war. Of course! But there are some kids who just do very well in a military situation. Don't you think Jordy is like that? Smart as a whip but all that spinning his wheels, doing poorly in school, here and there—do you hear from him?"

"He's not much for writing letters," I told her.

"Well honey, whenever you do, you tell him Billy and I send our love, and that we're praying for him. It would just kill Lily if something happened to that boy."

"You know, Rocky Perreira had a lot to do with Jordy becoming a pilot," I said. "And now getting on with Air America. Rocky's always been a big help to Jordy."

"Isn't that just so like Rocky, though? Such a big heart, and that way he has of making everybody enjoy themselves. Rocky is someone you always want on your guest list. Listen, I think making friends with him really helped your mother figure out how to handle it—when she was so new to things, and you know—at sea."

"I always thought it was you who helped mom out, Gladys. Her role model."

"Me? Don't be silly. What did I ever do that Lily could have learned from, except manage the servants? And with that marvelous cook of hers in charge of the household—What? Hsiu, of course—she didn't even have that to worry about. Listen, give Lily my love, will you? I can't even remember when we last saw each other. Don't they have a home leave coming up this year? There are so many people here who would just adore seeing them. I'll throw a party."

* * *

The weather has been gorgeous—like Miami at its best. With our doors and windows open we can hear music from an outdoor drama playing nearby, a touring group performing traditional opera. They set up a makeshift stage in the street, with little in the way of scenery. But the actors are elaborately gowned and made-up, with much of the make-up being bright red and snow white. The musicians sit on the stage attired in shirt-sleeves or undershirts and seem to play in random bursts every few minutes or during any of the action. The audience stands in front of the stage, and many of the little kids sit or stand right up on the stage, or else on their fathers' shoulders. The audience attire runs to bare feet, strapped-on babies, and scabby heads. The actors are very graceful and seem extremely sure of themselves and the parts they are playing. They act with gusto. The musicians, on the other hand, seem quite indifferent and sit on the stage, chatting, smoking, chewing and spitting betel nut, or scratching themselves. Although, they do always seem to come in on cue. I think. The actors never seem surprised, at least.

* * *

In November, about six weeks after we arrived in Taipei, Lilly wrote: *Through a girl in Sid's office, we met a native Taiwanese fellow who, for some unknown reason, is called Scotty by the Americans. Scotty speaks English and Mandarin and Taiwanese— he is the director of a school that teaches English—so he is a very useful fellow to go around with. He has taken us to outdoor markets, temples. Some are in very old parts of Taipei—down alleys so narrow even pedicabs can't get through, and we have to walk. We're always attracting attention and lot of stares, of course. But incidentally, I haven't sensed even the slightest negative feelings toward us from the people we encounter on the street for being Americans. Only curiosity and friendly smiles.*

On the other hand, there is quite a lot of resentment between the Taiwanese and the Chinese Nationalists who came here and took over when China went Red—and I imagine rightly so. The Mainland Chinese look down on the Taiwanese. I suppose it was really only those with money who made it out, and they probably feel marooned among the hicks now. The other night, Scotty was at our house for dinner and it seemed to me that the air was quite charged when Hsiu had to serve him. Their roles being reversed, I suppose you could say. Of course, the Taiwanese speak Chinese, but theirs is a completely different dialect than Mandarin, which the Govt. has adopted as the official language. Then they also had the Japanese occupation here for 50-some years until the end of the war.

Anyway, last Sunday we went with Scotty to a magnificent temple way up on a mountainside overlooking the city. We were given a special tour by a nun with a shaven head. At intervals, we were asked to be seated and were served tea. The kids were very impressed. Incidentally, tea is usually served here in glasses and is the jasmine type with flowers floating around in it. It's very charming to see and smell, but difficult to drink.

Speaking of the kids, the other day, Sid took them to a nearby
boatyard. They were accompanied by a sailing enthusiast, a fellow
who's here with the Embassy who has had a sloop built. He is trying
to interest some of the teenagers in sailing and has an idea of
building some type of little sailboats for the kids. Our kids seem
mildly intrigued, but Sid is enthused—probably thinks it's a chance
to make up for having been tied to a desk in the war, never mind
he was in the Navy. This sailing guy is an interesting character, I
understand—grew up in Macau, has lived all over the world,
speaks dozens of languages. People speak very highly of him.

* * *

This sailing guy.

Makes me picture Rocky soaring through the air, oddly,
not over the surface of the water. That was her first mention of
him, which surprised me, Rocky having ultimately been so
important to her. Had she even met him yet? Surely so, but only
in a crowd? Though we hadn't been there for long when she
wrote that, so maybe not.

All that mention of social events brought this to mind:
Lily, in bra and slip, working herself into a panic as she gets
ready for some official function. She has nothing to wear!
Discarded outfits pile up on the bed. Nothing looks right.
Nothing fits. Has she gained weight already? It is Hsiu's fault
with his goddamned tempting baked goods! She can't go! Sid
will have to go without her! She wishes we'd never come here.
My father says her name slowly, "Lilian," almost growling, with
the hint of an interrogative rise at the end. We know this tone
well. With just the name of whichever of us it was aimed at, Sid

could convey both "I'm warning you," and "Are you listening to me?" He didn't wait for her to answer. "Of course you're going. The car will be here. Put something on." Another husband might have said, "Sweetheart, you look terrific in the green. Wear the green. Wear the green with the pearls and you'll be the best-dressed woman there." Or even just, "Stop being ridiculous, you're fine in the green." But my father never used three words when one would do; any diplomatic skills he may have had were not squandered at home. Regardless, Lily always emerged perfectly turned out. She did have flair.

And she never did gain an ounce.

* * *

There's only one letter in which Lily felt compelled to resort to all caps.

November 9, 1957
Dearest Esther,

I was so thrilled to finally hear from you—the next best thing to talking in person. Even tho we have really loved and enjoyed every minute so far—and to you I wouldn't embroider—still I got a pang when I read all your news. I sometimes think, two years, ye gods. Actually, we only have another 22 months here AND I AM GOING TO ENJOY EVERY SECOND OF IT IF IT KILLS ME, DAMN IT. It's so fascinating, and I know I can't do it justice in these feeble letters, but I promise I'll tell you every single detail when it's over.

Anyway, I am beginning to find myself rather busy. Two days a week I help out in a thrift shop, the proceeds of which go toward youth activities in the American community. It is located at the Army PX and it's very pleasant to spend time there because everyone stops in to chat and visit—you see, people are always going to the PX to see what has come in since they were there the day before. So I'm meeting just about everybody.

The other day, I agreed to accompany Barbara van Kirk, the wife of Sid's boss, on a visit to a leprosarium with a committee that had collected some old clothes to distribute. It was a harrowing experience, to say the least—and we actually only saw the cases who were well enough to be up and around. I was more disturbed however, by van Kirk herself, who it turns out is one of those typical do-gooders, the type that makes you cringe. She made a darling little speech, which I hope was not translated literally, in which she said, "Be happy everybody, be happy with whatever you get," among other charming clichés. And here these miserable creatures were without fingers or toes with their faces all caved in. Then she had the lepers file out one by one while we handed each of them some garment at random.

Lauren came with me, too. She has been very much affected by the poverty and has been asking what someone like her could do. Well, she practically had hysterics in the car on the way home and spent the rest of the afternoon curled up on her bed. I was sick to my stomach about the whole thing and wouldn't have gone had I known it would be handled that way. And I'd certainly not taken my sensitive girl with me. I haven't been able to look at this van Kirk dame since. Although, I will have to force myself at some point. Well, we all know the type. I guess you can't escape them no matter how far you travel.

On a lighter topic, re your mother's kind inquiry as to the type of stove we have, tell her, how should I know? I have only set foot into the kitchen about three times since our arrival. Seriously, it is a coal stove, and I wouldn't have the faintest idea of how to cook on it or in it—I haven't even boiled water. Wait til I teach Hsiu how to make lokshen kugel and chopped liver.

Love from Your Foreign Correspondent

* * *

I promise I'll tell you every single detail when it's over. Only she never did.

Even as she missed her friends and felt torn about being away for the two years, Lily was engaged and amused. She described numerous sightseeing expeditions guided by Scotty, the Taiwanese guy from the language school, while accompanied by Coletta Robinson, the ICA secretary who had introduced him to us. We went to temples, which even in the general shabbiness of Taipei at the time were always tidily kept and were resplendent with color and precise detail. At one, we witnessed an unsettling ceremony involving hundreds of young boys, all dressed identically in black and white, holding big wooden swords and moving with choreographed martial precision. We shopped the street markets and Hagglers' Row, a lane crammed-full of antiques stalls. We hiked to visit monasteries up in the mountains and toured a hushed museum full of ancient porcelain and calligraphies.

Lily loved these expeditions. She greeted every person she could, asking questions and absorbing responses, with Scotty translating. Invariably, she would be dressed in a light-colored, full-skirted cotton shirtwaist, sleeves rolled up above her elbows, collar opened to the second button. A simple, breezy sort of outfit that, despite the mostly humid weather, might as well have borne the legend "Never Wilts" on its label. How she managed to always appear fresh and cool is a mystery to me. She might as well have been a practitioner of one of those philosophies asserting that concept that however you picture yourself inwardly will be reflected in your outward reality. Lily reported it all with enthusiasm. At the end of one such jaunt, she mentions this: *We then visited Coletta in her tiny house—it is a Japanese type and utterly charming—with sliding panels and a precious little garden with rocks and pebbles. She's quite an interesting girl herself.* There's no word of Rocky during these weeks.

What I didn't remember—or maybe didn't notice since, at the time, it seemed perfectly normal to me—was her consciousness of us as Jews. *We set out with Ella and Henry Mitnick and their two kids for a spot called Green Lake. Incidentally, I must say I'm surprised to find this many Jews on the scene, since the diplomatic community overall is quite gentile in style and manners. What do I mean? Reserved, I guess? Which Ella certainly is not. Very inquisitive, and also very nervous. But they invited us, our kids and theirs get along. What can you do? Anyway, we rented some boats, which looked a bit like Italian gondolas. Each came with a man who ferries you up and down the lake. I felt like Cleopatra being transported down the Nile. I don't know how that little old guy did it, either. He stands at one end with a 20-foot pole that he uses to push the boat along and, after some considerable haggling, he ends up doing so for the equivalent of about 30 cents an hour. While we were out, a storm blew up, so he pulled us to shore where some enterprising fellow who speaks a little*

English has a couple of bamboo shanties overlooking the water. You can rent them for overnite or for the afternoon, if you wish—he calls it the Little Sea Hut, and it has a very romantic atmosphere. Not a bad idea for a hideaway.

Anyhoo, Ella talked me into throwing a Chanukah party at our house for all the Jewish people we could round up. I wondered why she didn't host it herself. I certainly don't want her to get the idea that I'll jump into whatever project she's got in mind for me. But to be fair, she's already on a million committees, and with Hsiu and Wei, it's really no work to entertain. We had about 25 adults and 12 children. Lauren made a terrific mobile with figures of boys and girls dancing the Hora, and Jordy even forgot to be a prickly teenager for a few minutes and pitched in with the decorating. We served potato latkes—I showed Hsiu how to make them and they were wonderful—with sour cream, which is now, Hallelujah, available at the PX, and all the other usual things. There were a couple of boys present who are here studying on Ford Foundation fellowships, and one of them lives with a Chinese family and eats only Chinese food. Well, he almost burst into tears when he saw the sour cream—he just couldn't get enuf.

Then, on Christmas day, Gladys and Billy from next door invited our family to breakfast. It turned out to be a large party with several other families and a very elegant champagne brunch—if you can imagine champagne at 10 a.m. That was certainly new to us, but I could develop a taste for it if I had to.

* * *

An afternoon boating party, though it didn't exactly take place on a boat. Rocky had access to a sort of barge that was truly just a big, rough platform floating on pontoons. It was furnished with some aluminum and webbing lawn chairs and an umbrella; some people sat around on coolers. There was no railing around the edge, which in retrospect is pretty risky since there were many boisterous kids present. Lily wrote, *We didn't actually go anywhere, just stayed tied up at the boatyard where Rocky moors his sailboat. But it was the craziest thing—all these Americans acting as if they were having a cookout in somebody's Silver Spring backyard, while the life of the river passed us by— people out there were hauling coal and gravel in their little boats, fishermen unloading their catches, and what must have been the entire riverside neighborhood, from old grannies to little toddlers wearing only t-shirts, were all lined up along the wharf to watch us.*

This must have been in winter, maybe four or five months after we arrived in Taipei, because I remember a mild, radiant day, not the city's sledgehammer tropical summer. Sid was acting effusive, as if he loved a party, although I don't think he normally did. While passing around drinks with Dyson van Kirk and Rocky, he spoke loudly for everybody to hear. "Every temple we visit, Lily tosses some coins into the collection box. Confucian, Buddhist, God forbid we ever get to Europe, there are churches in every plaza I'm told. She'll break the bank."

Even though pretending not to hear, Lily sparkled at being made the center of attention. Even in this backhanded way, even while being portrayed as frivolous. It was she who delivered the punch line after a pause of two beats—was this a script they'd rehearsed? She said, "Well you just never know. There's no collection plate in a synagogue, but one way or another, I'm making sure I get to heaven." There were a few mild chuckles, and she added brightly, "Of course, Jews don't really worry much about going to Hell, we've had so much of it here on Earth."

Rocky laughed out loud and cuffed Sid on the shoulder, as if they were great buddies. He said, "Hang on to *her*," or something like that. Ella Mitnick seemed to squirm. No one spoke for a moment until Gladys drawled in her ironic, maternal way, "Oh, honey, let's make it a rule to never talk about religion, politics, or money. Except for how much anybody has—money, that is."

Barbara van Kirk emitted one of her quick, tight, three-beat laughs. The van Kirks were Catholic. I had a misimpression of Catholics at this stage in my sheltered life, which was reinforced by Mrs. van Kirk's personality. I felt that Catholics' distinguishing characteristic was emotional repression. Or their fondness for suffering, something like that. I hardly knew anything about what made Catholics tick, if that's something that can even be defined. I took it as further evidence toward my belief the fact that the van Kirks did not send their daughters—Haven and Barbara, who was called Babby to distinguish her from her mother—to the big International School we attended. It had a bracing mix of nationalities and, I suppose, religions too. But it also had American-style basketball games and cheerleaders and Saturday night dances in the gym and kids going steady, with girls getting pinned and lavaliered, and felt up, and some probably getting laid, as well. No, Haven and Babby attended an institution run by somber Irish nuns, in a clammy building with a mud courtyard. Maybe it wasn't always muddy, but it was the one time I'd seen the school. At Lily's insistence, I had attended a Christmas recital there, which Haven was singing in. Haven and I weren't close, but because she was my age, any time we were both present she and I were expected to be friends. Now the two of us were sitting on the edge of the floating platform with our feet dangling over, making a bored game out of avoiding the polluted river water. My toenails were painted a hot coral at Lily's urging. Haven's were just ten little pinkish blanks.

Now that I think about it, I would have been facing out with a view over the water, or else toward the congested riverbank and the continually shifting crowd of onlookers. *You have to get used to being stared at by friendly but very curious eyes at any and all times,* Lily wrote. If the people on the bank were staring at us, and I was looking at them, I couldn't very well have noted the expressions and responses this routine of Sid and Lily's evinced among the members of our boating party. Or was it a routine of Sid and Lily and Rocky's?

Maybe I'm making up the dialogue, too.

And now that I am wondering about the accuracy of my recollection, I'm thinking Ella and Henry probably weren't even there. I don't remember the Mitnicks being much a part of the social whirl, as Lily called it. Were they a bit *too* Jewy? Did that mean Lily and Sid, on the contrary, could pass? Or maybe the Mitnicks just weren't much fun. It occurrs to me that at 15 and 16, I might not have been involved enough in the social whirl myself to know how they were perceived. Maybe I'm beginning to confabulate memories from a mixture of the bits I do recall, the things Lily wrote in her letters or sometime mentioned to me in some offhand way, and the expectations of how I think things ought to have been. Or must have been. I remember that Ella had this anxious habit, rubbing the heel of her palm in a circle against the side of her head. She didn't let their kids go around the city by pedicab or bicycle on their own, as most of the parents did. *The American kids just run wild all over the city, but nobody would dare touch them,* Lily had written, then repeated something I'm sure she'd heard Sid say, *because the people are just grateful to have us here instead of the Reds.* It was possible Ella was over-sensitive to dangers and slights, or perhaps she was simply aware of the real ones that came from being Jewish. Unlike Lily, whose heedlessness—or pretense of heedlessness—functioned as her armor, which enhanced her charm.

As further evidence that the Mitnicks weren't there, they never did get one of those little sailboats. There were a lot of children at this floating party because Rocky was using it to recruit families to build these boats. You have to wonder what was in this for him. He already had his beautiful big sloop. There were all kinds of things he could have spent his free time doing. He loved a party, never seemed to tire of them, so maybe this was a way to guarantee festive weekend afternoons that would then segue into the more typical cocktail soirees and dinner events. Or maybe he just loved kids and families and wanted to surround himself with them. He certainly involved himself with ours. Kids loved him, that's for sure.

Rocky had a couple of coolies carry a prototype of the little boat down to the water from the shed where he'd had it built. He took kids out one at a time for quick spins. There was a decent breeze, steady but not too strong. "We were flying!" Jordy enthused when his turn was over and he was clambering back up onto the barge. Was that brief boat ride alone with Rocky when Jordy's enchantment, or infatuation, with him began? Sid had a boat ride, too. With him aboard, Rocky took a longer circuit than any of the kids got, twice across the wide river and back. The two men could be seen, though not heard, in conversation, and when my father stepped up out of the little dinghy, they seemed quite pally. "Well, Jordan," Sid asked my brother. "Shall we have one of these yachts built, too?" We did get one, of course. And all of us learned a few rudiments of sailing from Rocky, including Sidney Norell, ex-Navy. All of us but Lily. I believe it was a different kind of skill she picked up from Rocky.

Sid always maintained a friendship with Rocky. At least, they maintained the appearance of a friendship. I don't think of my father as having had particularly warm friendships with other men. He wasn't a warm person, and he didn't live during a time when that type of thing easily happened. Maybe his "friends" were the guys he went off doing whatever with when he was off doing mysterious things. But there was no reason he couldn't love Rocky or be seen to love Rocky. Everybody loved Rocky. It's interesting that the two of them had such different personalities, since they were engaged in the same kind of work. If they were, I mean. If Rocky was running agents, I imagine he would have been paternal toward them, cosseting, forgiving, wheedling maybe, but subtly so. If Sid was running agents, he would have been all about precision and discipline. But I'm imagining all that too. Their nefarious doings. How would I possibly know?

* * *

Dear Rosie,

Just received your letter and loved every word. Almost as if you were talking to me in person. So please, please write, even if there's no news. It brings you all closer. This is not my regular bulletin, I just felt like answering right away. The people here are simply charming, but I haven't met anybody yet whom I can really let my hair down with. If I could only come and see you all once or twice a year, it would be perfect. The two years—well, only 19 months now—stretch ahead like infinity.

But honestly, we are having a really fine time and life is so very pleasant and relaxed and easy. Sid is working very hard and often has meetings or tasks in the evenings if we don't have a social engagement. Even when he comes home for lunch, he can be preoccupied. Had I mentioned that he is driven home for lunch every day at noon and picked up again at 1? He loves the work, and all the higher-ups seem very pleased with him, too.

Jordy is often out exploring with his friend Tommy Church from two doors down, who seems to know all the things of interest to do and see, since the Churches have been in Taipei for three years now. The boys often ride bikes to the airport, where they can even go into some of the parked planes and sit in the cockpits. When Jordy divulged that they race their bikes down the runway, Sid nearly had a breakdown. But there are only a few flights in and out every day, thank God, and I have to assume the airport personnel shoo them off when one is about to land.

Sid and the kids are enthused about this project of building sailboats, which a fellow at the Embassy came up with. These will be tiny things, eight-foot dinghies, apparently very easy to sail and perfect for kids to learn on. The type of boat is called an "El Toro," which means "the bull" in Spanish. Its symbol, which will be on the sail of each one, is a shovel, as in shoveling the b_____t—a joke about their small size, which apparently all boating types will instantly find amusing. About ten families are having them built. The men involved decided over drinks to form the Taipei International Yacht and Racing Association—another joke, when you picture these tiny things. Lauren had the clever idea of naming our boat "Dinghy Hau," which is yet another little joke, because "ding hau" is how you say "very good" in Chinese. I suppose we will return home with detailed knowledge of all things nautical which people like you and me, who grew up in cities and sprang from the poor Jews of Europe, never encountered before. When our tour here is over, we may just have to move to Annapolis and get new wardrobes and a sloop and an entirely new set of friends—goyim all.

Yesterday, when Sid was home for lunch, he started going on about how ideal this life is for us, how much money we are able to save with so many of our expenses paid for by the government—and that he wants to remain overseas for the rest of his career. That could be 25 years. The thought fills me with gloom. When he went back to work, I simply lost control. Wei, the amah, found me sobbing. She was beside herself in trying to cheer me up and understand what was wrong, and of course she and I can barely communicate, so in the end it was really quite funny. I was desperate to tell her everything was "Okay," and she patted me and hugged me and repeated "Oh, missy," in a distressed voice, and we ended up laughing it all off. But that didn't leave me feeling any better. I guess you can't have everything, so pls., take vitamins & stay good and healthy for our return so we can have plenty of those late coffee-drinking sessions and fill each other in. God willing, we will really be coming home at the end of this tour, and not just for two months of home leave before returning here or moving on to whatever other corner of the globe Sid and Uncle Sam come up with next.

* * *

The ICA men generally dressed down for the office, wearing open-necked short-sleeve shirts, due to the lack of air conditioning where they worked. To dress up for more formal events, Sid always wore a bow tie. I don't remember anybody else wearing a bow tie. It was a deliberate quirk, like a coded message that insisted there was something different going on with him—and there was, I am pretty sure now. Something nobody was officially allowed to know, but which anybody who wanted to might have noticed. On his boat, Rocky usually wore Bermuda shorts, equally unconventional for the day, and which perhaps had the same function, except that Rocky in shorts seemed natural, while Sid in bow ties seemed self-conscious.

Anyway, I have this vivid memory, although it is surely a conflation of many similar moments in that house in Taipei: It is early evening. My parents are getting ready to leave to attend some social function. Lily is a bit disorganized and runs a few minutes late while getting dressed and making up. Sid paces back and forth outside along the garden wall that is thickly curtained with allamanda vines, the caramel-yellow blossoms of which are losing color in the dusk. Then Lily emerges, wearing one of those perfectly put-together cocktail ensembles and a thoroughly unrushed look that refuses to acknowledge any fact of delay. He never says a word about it, either; his jaw is clenched. When they go to the car, he opens her door for her, gets in himself behind the wheel, nods to Hsiu to open the gate, and they drive away.

Actually, Sid did accept a second tour in Taipei, from '59 to '61. That's when the Kennedy administration came into office and changed the name of the State Department unit Sid worked for; the ICA, International Cooperation Administration, became the AID, Agency for International

54

Development. Which made perfect sense to us. USAID: We were the helping hand of a government that generously extended across the globe, or so we smugly thought. Passing out cast-offs to lepers. Teaching interrogation tactics to police forces in authoritarian states, as was revealed some years later. It's easy to be cynical now, but at the time we didn't think it had to do with politics or intrigue. I didn't, anyway. And Lily, too, seemed oblivious to those nuances. Although the agency's earlier name, which had been replaced with ICA, was FOA, Foreign Operations Administration. The chilling opacity of that ought to have given us a hint.

During his tours in Taiwan, Sid was often sent on temporary assignments to Laos and Vietnam. Then in '61 he was actually reassigned to the AID mission in Vietnam, and he and Lily moved to Saigon. They had two tours there and by the time they were transferred again—this time to Bangkok in '65—the Vietnam War was well underway, unmistakable in its grim promise to anyone who cared to look, which did not include myself, or my mother for that matter. After two tours in Thailand, they were transferred to Jakarta, where they stayed for three. Sid ended up staying in the Foreign Service, just as he'd wanted.

But things would change for Lily by the time that first tour in Taipei was over. She would find something she was passionate about and effective at, and which she could carry on with and be lauded for at each successive post. And she would stop feeling lonely. She made friends in those first years in Taipei, a few of whom she stayed close with for the rest of her life.

Foreign Service folk are always being reassigned and running into each other again somewhere else down the line.

How lucky for Lily, for example, that Rocky Perreira had a career that also had him moving around Asia, where he would frequently cross paths with her during all those years to come.

My parents ended up very far from their origins, and not only in miles. Both were the children of Eastern European immigrants and spent their childhoods in working-class New York neighborhoods, where they knew virtually no one who wasn't Jewish and where, for the majority who were not Orthodox, leftism of various hues and stripes dominated peoples' worldviews. Lily's father died young, and she grew up with her mother and her father's sister Minna in a one-bedroom apartment in Brooklyn. From my perspective as an adult with a privileged childhood, it seems like a pretty awkward menage, but they were used to making do. The steamy closeness and good-natured kvetching and Yiddish accents of that Brooklyn household, along with my Gramma's traditional cooking, were savory treats whenever we visited from our roomy split-level in suburban Bethesda. It was as entertaining as visiting another country.

Gramma kept house in that cramped apartment, while Aunt Minna went out to work as a sewing machine operator. She was also an activist in the garment workers' union. And she was also perhaps a member of the Communist Party, though my parents only whispered about that detail, usually with a frown. Those were the red-baiting Fifties, after all. They were in Washington, and Sid was in government, and they must have feared the label. Minna always insisted that she was being followed and that her mail was opened by the FBI, a claim that my father scornfully belittled to her face, even if he might have been nervous it was true. And who knows?

Sid's family was neither religious nor political, and were thus outliers in that world. Perhaps this was the source of his own studied individualism, his need to forever identify himself as existing outside of the crowd. Maybe it accounts for his sartorial quirk of wearing only bow ties, and for his rarely ever voting—and when he did, sometimes voting Republican—and for his making a career in the Foreign Service when its reception of Jews was still chilly. It intrigues me that in adulthood, it was Sid who became political and an agent of American foreign policy—possibly even a secret agent—and that Lily was the one who always seemed totally unconcerned with politics.

In any case, both of them were strivers. She wrote that Sid was eager to have a sailboat built when Rocky was promoting the idea. Although I clearly recall Lily helping convince *him* to get one by pointing out that several influential people were also doing it, and that the little meets and regattas on the water would provide her and Sid a way to get connected.

* * *

I can recall the way Lily spoke. Her voice sounds in my head as I read through the letters. It surprises me that they are so peppered with Yiddish and with figures of speech in English that I think of as Jewish. Like a lot of Jewish-Americans in my generation, I was used to hearing our American-born parents bumble along in Yiddish. They grew up hearing it since it was their own parents' first language. But people like Lily and Sid weren't really fluent, and only used it with their elder relatives. Or as a secret code between themselves when they didn't want the kids to understand what they were saying. Whatever few expressions I knew and may even have occasionally uttered as a kid, I forgot long ago. For some reason, now, I only remember the names of Jewish foods, most of which I can barely picture anymore. Kichel. Or kuchel? Kugel? Farfel. Tzimmes—something with carrots? Reading the letters now feels as if I am having a refresher course.

It's not just Lily's use of Yiddish, either. There's a vocabulary that fixes her to a moment in history—a combination of American cultural history and Jewish immigrant history—a vocabulary arrayed along a spectrum of assimilation from self-conscious to self-assured, anxious to ambitious, marginal to mainstream. Lily didn't think twice about using words like stunning or darling or heavenly. Her Aunt Minna would never have uttered them. For Minna, something was pretty or nice—or nice-enough-leave-it-at-that. Aunt Minna had a brusque leftist proletarian contempt for anything inessential, or as she would have put it, fancy-schmancy. Despite the deliberately cramped lexicon, she was fluent in English with only the slightest foreign accent, which was more a distinction of cadence than of pronunciation, since she'd immigrated as a little girl and gone through public school in New York.

Lily and her Bethesda friends were entirely at home in the postwar era of suburbanization and economic boom, though, being lavish consumers and avid enthusiasts of its culture. Fearlessly and unthinkingly, they used American words and expressions their parents either wouldn't have known or wouldn't have felt entitled to. They said *stunning* and *darling* and *heavenly* as confidently as they steered their tanklike Mercuries and Studebakers to the gleaming new Giant supermarket, just as they attended League of Women Voters meetings with their gentile neighbors and signed up to be poll watchers. They felt that they belonged. But there was also language they would only use among themselves, winkingly, intimately. *Haimishly*, to transmute a Yiddish adjective into an English adverb—there's one word I do remember. They lapsed for moments into actual Yiddish and used constructions like "we should only live so long" and "to you I wouldn't lie."

Even when she'd become a deracinated cosmopolitan Foreign Service wife, surely she still had that Yiddish-inflected, first-generation American way of speaking? I can't recall. People often change the way they speak when they reinvent themselves. So maybe not, by the time she was in her eighties, sipping gimlets on her terrace in Hong Kong. Those last few times I saw her, she still spoke in the first voice I had ever known. At the time, I wasn't trying to understand my mother. I still had a rather uncomfortable relationship with her. I wasn't really even hearing her—not in the way I am hearing her now, as I read the letters. But now there is no more conversation, only these flimsy scraps that could scatter and crumble with the slightest touch of a breeze.

* * *

Rosie dear—

Today we received your package—five weeks after it was postmarked. Surface mail takes forever, but it would have cost a fortune by air, and splurge like that you shouldn't. In any case, the rugelach survived mostly intact. They were so welcomed by all, which brought us thoughts of you and made me miss home terribly.

Rose was a terrific cook, particularly of Eastern European Jewish standards. Kreplach, gefilte fish, blintzes. "My mother's matzo balls are like rocks," Lily would repeat annually at Rose's Passover table—after the ritual's four glasses of wine; she hadn't been much of a drinker before the Foreign Service. "But Rosie, yours are little pillows. Simply divoon!" *Incidentally, please send me your recipe for stuffed cabbage. I ought to start reciprocating after all the affairs we've been invited to. I think I will give a series of smallish dinners. Maybe one with all Jewish-type stuff. People might enjoy something a little different. Although, it depends which people. You get the feeling that one or two would hesitate to put their fork into any food they knew was ours.*

Now that I think about it, Rose was a foodie before the concept existed. She was the first person I knew who served pasta with anything other than tomato sauce and used fresh garlic rather than garlic salt from a jar. Garlic salt is a good metaphor for Lily's aptitude for domestic arts. Lily hated cooking and loved all things "modern" and "labor-saving," from Redi-Whip to the garbage disposal in the sink. In Bethesda, Jordy and I consumed TV Dinners on folding tray tables in front of the television on the many nights when Sid was late coming home. When there was no command-performance family gathering around the dining table. There we were, eating in flickering blue light with no parent in evidence—another metaphor—which still did not make the two of us allies much of the time, or even particularly good friends. Well, TV Dinners would be a sad basis for intimacy. For a long time, I have thought of our family as whirling apart after we went to Taipei, but maybe we were already on our separate trajectories before that.

Lily only ever wanted to cook things that were more or less foolproof. Meat loaf, potato salad, chopped liver, coleslaw. Her flourish was to sprinkle them all with paprika, stale paprika of unknown provenance bought at the Giant in little rectangular cans. It was not to add any flavor, since it had none, but rather to pretty things up with a powdery dusting of red. She taught Hsiu to do that, too. One of her favorite anecdotes, toward the end, was about a day shortly after they had moved to Jakarta. There being no U.S. military PX there, neatly packaged industrial American foods were wholly unavailable. At the market, Hsiu had found—amid the perfect pyramids of crimson, gold, and rust-colored seeds and spices and curry blends—brilliant, scarlet ground paprika. He strewed it over everything he served for dinner that evening. "Ha. Ha. Ha," Lily would say, pretending to enjoy having been the butt of an accidental joke. "Who ever thought of paprika as pepper? I was breathing fire. For a minute, Hsiu turned me into a dragon lady." When she told this story, Hsiu would stand nearby with his tray, a coy smile on his lips.

Lily herself never baked. In our Bethesda house, any baking was done by our Black maid Bathsheba, who had come up from Georgia and sometimes fixed Southern recipes that she knew by heart—cornbread, cobblers, pies. Bathsheba made a very nice pie crust. Lily, of course, famously never ate dessert. People groaned at her standard line when dessert was offered: "You know I never touch sweets." But I recall her often enough lunching on a slender shard of Bathsheba's sweet potato pie— though it was always topped with a scoop of cottage cheese instead of ice cream. "Sweet potato is a vegetable," she would insist.

Rosie, in the same mail was a letter from Jeannette, who mentions something about Louis Cantor—I can't even bring myself to type it—and she evidently assumes that I know the facts. I just can't believe that such a thing is true, and I am hoping against hope that perhaps she is misinformed. I have been sunk in the worst gloom all day—I feel so helpless and so far away from you all. Please, please let me know all the facts <u>at once</u>. I only hope that the tears I have shed have been for nothing, but I am afraid that Jeannette wouldn't write such a horrible thing if it weren't so. In your letter, you mentioned seeing Clara in the Safeway, so if anything did happen to Louis, it must have been very sudden. I wanted to try and call Clara or write to her—but I felt that I should first find out if it really were so. I couldn't feel worse if it were someone in my own family, believe me. There must be some pattern or reason behind these things. I only wish we had a faint glimmer of what it is.

Sid and I have just come back from attending a Girl Scout banquet with Lauren, and if ever I was not in the mood for Girl Scouts, this was it. But no matter what happens, or how badly we feel, we all go on doing what we have to, and we go right on living. If this tragic news is true, then I know you and Essie are doing all you can for Clara. I will write her, but what is there to say? In the last analysis, when there is trouble, you have to face it all alone. I will be anxiously waiting to hear from you, doll—

Love you and miss you,
Lily

* * *

Dearest Esther,

I received your most welcome letter yesterday—and I am really heartbroken about Louis. It simply seems unbelievable to us. I have just finished writing to Clara—but all the drivel you write doesn't really express what you feel. I just want to scream at Fate. We all know that death is inevitable and must face it one way or another—but how do you prepare for it when it comes so unexpectedly? The Chinese seem to have worked out a satisfactory philosophy. Their funerals are something to see. They have a group of musicians who walk in front of the cart that's carrying the coffin, which is entirely covered in flowers—it all seems gay rather than sad. They believe in a hereafter, so that if the person has led a good life on Earth, he will be on the way to a better one in the next world. I really wish I could believe that, don't you?

Please, God, that there won't be any more sad news while we are away, and that you are all there to greet us when we return. If I can get Sid to come home, that is. More than once, it's come up that we might stay in the Foreign Service.

* * *

All this about Louis Cantor's death makes me feel…well, sunk in the worst kind of gloom. But not about Louis, exactly, whom of course I knew but not as a peer. Just as one of the men in a large circle of grownups who were "our" friends because they were our parents' friends. It's the intensity of Lily's connection and longing for Esther and Rose and their community back home that moves me. Her involvement in these friendships that were only forged in full adulthood—which seems so late in life to achieve that type of relationship.

I have two or three lifelong friends from school and college whom I don't see or even communicate with often, but whom I treasure and connect well with when we do talk. Rosemary, from Taipei, and Cheryl Jacobs, who was my first and only roommate for four years at the University of Michigan. A totally random but felicitous connection, which resulted from a bureaucratic decision by some unknown employee in the housing office. I lost another dear friend from Michigan, Gary Rausch, to AIDS in the early Nineties before the development of the drugs that would have saved him. Oh, and I was married to a guy there, at Michigan. I always forget about that. Really, I do. But it only lasted a year. No, eleven months, and it's so long ago that it's as if it never even happened. To the extent that I recall, it was more like going steady with somebody for a time and then having it slowly dawn on me that he wasn't the one. I don't even know what went wrong, but I also couldn't tell you why we got together in the first place. Most likely it happened because we were both about to graduate and afraid of having to figure out what to do with ourselves next...Jeffrey Weinberg, whose middle name I have forgotten. Douglas, maybe? It's of no consequence, my brief marriage. Unless it has something to do with why I have essentially been single ever since. But he's not what I mean by a lifelong friend.

Anyway, once I was out of school and into the world, I never made another friend as close or lasting as these—ex-husband Weinberg not one of them, obviously. It's easy when you're in a world of students, and hard once you take on adult responsibilities. Of course, I've known a million people, more perhaps than most, since I've moved around so much and had so many different jobs, all of which had to do with what you might call customer service. This is, I suppose, a silly thing to be bothered by now that I am not far away from 80 and have ended up by choice in a city where I know virtually no one, and I no longer have a job, let alone one that is centered around interacting with endless queues of people.

But Lily's closeness with her friends makes me feel lonely. In retrospect. What exactly have I missed in my life? And why?

* * *

...*we were invited out boating by Rocky Perreira, the fellow who has convinced Sid and eight or ten others to have these little sailboats built. He is simply a gorgeous man. He's our cultural attaché, a confirmed bachelor, his family was originally Portuguese and he spent some of his childhood in Macau. Looks it too, very dark, a wonderful smile. I'm dying to get his story. Honestly, I sometimes feel that we are meeting the League of Nations. He speaks six languages, including Mandarin and Cantonese. He's learning Taiwanese, too. They're all different dialects, you know. Anyway, a number of us went out on his sloop down the river to a lovely spot where we had a picnic lunch. The kids got to hold the tiller and trim the sails and batten the hatches and had a fine old time. All in all, it was heavenly and the first time since I got the bad news about Louis that I didn't feel that terrible weight on my heart.*

* * *

They took each other in, over sandwiches, Lily and Rocky. And it was heavenly.

Let me tell you something about Rocky. Roque: it means rock. If he makes me think of a rock, it is a flat rock by the water's edge, where you might sprawl out in the hot sun, with your sailboat bobbing sweetly just a few yards away. A baby-naming website I visited to double-check the translation declares, "People with this name have a deep inner desire for travel and adventure, and want to set their own pace in life without being governed by tradition." You'll think I made that silliness up because it fits him so well, and because expecting a name to determine a personality is rather a stretch, but I didn't. Google it yourself.

Rocky taught us to sail. He gave us knowledge of that state of buoyant exhilaration, that luminous sensation of taut canvas whiteness—which is always edged with deep blue peril, sparkling green menace, the possibility of a gunwale tilting too far into the water, going under. Edged, because maybe the danger is only revealed as the ultramarine thread in the stitching of a sail's hem. Or else as a tinge, a darkening stain, seeping into the fabric. One minute you're flying along the waves, lungs full of wind and shouting, sprays of turquoise and jade droplets shooting far behind you. You don't see them hit the surface unless you twist around to look. But turn around once, and you might find yourself capsized and suddenly gasping for air.

Of course we capsized those little El Toros, even on gentle Green Lake where the water was warm and there were no waves. Rocky always reacted with a roar of laughter, arms shrugged wide as if to congratulate us for committing such a delightful mistake. And then he would fish us out and together we would right the dinghy. They were so small and light that Rocky and

66

any one of us kids were easily able to lift the draining hull and flip it back over. You felt privileged to be doing that together, momentarily rendered equal to this grownup who was so alluringly foreign, though not exactly a foreigner.

* * *

Lily was quickly acquiring the knack. In January, she gave her first real party as a bon voyage for Billy Walter who was headed back to Washington for some meetings. I don't think she had considered that Chanukah get together to be *hers*. That was something she did as a member of the tribe, while I suppose this was about stepping forward on her own. Maybe she had previously served Rose's stuffed cabbage, but now she had realized that Hsiu could produce the food, borrowing a second cook and a houseboy or two to set up tables and serve. That left her to concentrate on guest lists and seating charts, themes and menus, flowers, and what to wear. She had learned how cheaply she could have clothes custom-tailored. The first thing she ordered was a cheongsam, one of those long, snug Chinese dresses with the slit up the sides, cap sleeves, and a high collar closed by frogs. In violet brocade, it was very slinky.

She loved the rituals and encounters of having clothes made as much as the clothes themselves—picking out material, paging through magazines to see what "they" were wearing, the requisite series of fittings. *Gladys took me to the tailor she uses, and I was very pleased with his work. He calls himself Jackson and is much patronized by the Americans, altho he speaks not a word of English. His labels and bags all say very proudly, "Jackson &*

67

Country. Dresses & Making." I imagine he once saw Town & Country magazine. Isn't that a scream?

Later that month, Sid was sent to Vietnam for a couple of weeks of TDY, temporary duty. Why? What for, exactly? Lily wrote that it was an indication of how quickly he had *whipped things into shape at the mission* and was a promising marker of success at his job. Whatever that actually was.

* * *

Sid came back from Saigon obsessed with Asia, writ large. Or writ larger than Taipei. He'd had an overnight in Hong Kong too. His city-boy origins had been touched. "This place looks like a village in comparison," he said. *He keeps mentioning how lovely and beautiful the Vietnamese women are, for which I would have him sleeping in the garage if he hadn't also brought me a gorgeous* áo dài. *This is what they wear over there, an ankle-length tunic split at the sides over a sort of pajama pants. It's in a stunning fabric—pale blue silk with a silvery sheen, almost sheer, long sleeves and a stand-up collar, and the slacks are a matching color—tho not so transparent! Unfortunately, the top is too small for me—those Vietnamese girls must be on the willowy side. But we'll have the outfit altered to fit Lauren, and I plan to have it copied for myself if I can find a similar material. It will make a very striking cocktail costume.*

February was foggy and damp, the lanes slick with mud. It wasn't wintry cold, but no place, including our house, had central heating. The servants were off for several days on account of Chinese New Year. I guess Hsiu forgot to explain about the water heater, which was located in a closet off the kitchen courtyard and was fueled by coal. Unattended, it soon died out. Sid, being home alone at the time, went to investigate. To get it started up again he doused some coal with kerosene and tossed in a match. It'd either been too much kerosene, or he was just peering too closely into the firebox—but a burst of flame singed his face. He drove himself to the clinic at the U.S. Air Force base. It wasn't a very serious burn. They cleaned him up and wrapped his whole head in gauze like a mummy, with openings for his eyes, ears, nostrils and mouth. Lily wrote, *You know Sid, nothing is ever a problem. So he drove himself back through town like this. People on the streets stopped dead in their tracks, and some ran screaming as if it were a ghost at the wheel. The funniest part is that the Chinese actually call white people "ghosts" in their language. The bandages came off after a day. He's fine. But when poor Lauren came home and saw him with his head wrapped up like that, she had an absolute breakdown.*

In other news, we are now the owners of the fattest little puppy you ever did see. He was given to us by some people whose tour was over. He came to us as Bucky, but Jordy has renamed him Bomber.

* * *

On a mild Sunday in early March, we went for a picnic. Along with us were my classmate Rosemary, Jordy's friend Tommy, Coletta, and Scotty. The little dog joined too. Scotty's English was very good, if not especially fluid, and that slight awkwardness undermined his apparent desire to project a sporty American affect. He smoked Lucky Strikes in a breezy way that was probably copied from movies, and I only ever saw him wearing short sleeve polo shirts with those little alligator logos.

That struck me as funny, because before we left for Taiwan, when Lily was filling out our wardrobes, she'd bought a dozen of them for Jordy, one in every color. He resisted wearing them. They were too conformist, I guess, too preppy, although that wasn't a word yet, for the other boys he wanted to impress. Scotty guided us to a place on Grass Mountain where, during their occupation, the Japanese had made lovely, secluded gardens with pebbled pathways and stone benches. There was a bridge arching over a little stream and long views down toward the city. I thought it was enchanting. Scotty said, "It is not so tidy as the Japanese would have it, but while they were here, we were not allowed in this place. This garden was for their chiefs only."

Now, the park was full of Chinese families on a weekend outing. We attracted the usual curious attention. Lily wrote, *And if you speak a word or two in Chinese, they are delighted. Sid now knows quite a few words and so does Lauren, who is taking an after-school class and has made friends with a local girl in her same year at the International School, Rosemary Ling, the daughter of a vice-minister of Defense. I am starting a Chinese conversation class myself, as a matter of fact. A Chinese lady is going to teach six women some phrases that are necessary in the life of the average American wife, such as, "Is that a genuine antique or a fake?" and "Do you have Revlon's Fire & Ice nail polish?" Unfortunately, the language has four tones, and the meanings of a word vary depending on the tone you use. The fact that I am utterly non-musical will surely be a problem, but I feel morally obligated to try in the interest of good international relations. Jordy is learning some Chinese too, although the extent of it is mostly curse words and slang expressions—Scotty was scandalized when he and Tommy rattled them off. It was a panic.*

Incidentally Coletta Robinson, the girl from Sid's agency who introduced us to Scotty, was with us. She is another very unusual person. She's a Negro—the only one here in the diplomatic community that I know of, tho of course we see colored boys at the Air Force base, where we go to use the pool and library. She grew up in Oakland, California, where she knew a lot of Chinese people as neighbors and just developed a fascination with all things Chinese. She went to college at Berkeley, where she majored in Chinese language. That must certainly have been a help in her getting hired at State, considering. To end up posted here in Taiwan is a dream come true for her. She is the executive secretary to the Mission Director, responsible for things like making appointments with the various ministries and making sure the locally hired secretaries know what they're doing. She met Scotty when she went to arrange English classes for the motor pool drivers. She and Scotty can chatter away in Chinese, and it's rather odd to hear that from a Negro—but then her English is extremely well-spoken too, and if you only talked with her on the phone you wouldn't think she was different at all. She's simply a lovely and interesting person, and I'm surprised we don't see her out more at social gatherings. She's single, and maybe isn't always invited to things because of it—it's mostly all couples here, of course.

The little sailboats have all been completed and judged seaworthy. Ours is painted a rather jaunty yellow and blue. It's adorable. I personally do not plan to ever step aboard, having discovered en route across the Pacific that I prefer vessels with the size and luxuries of the S. S. Lurline. I understand that Brad Mencken, Vice Pres. of Civil Air Transport—charming guy, whom we've met—keeps a perfectly comfortable cabin cruiser on the river, from the deck of which I will be happy to observe; the Lurline it ain't, but he is renowned for his onboard cocktail bar. Civil Air Transport—CAT—is one of the few airlines that flies here. It was started by some of the Flying Tigers, that American pilot squadron who stuck around on the Mainland after the war. And then when the Nationalists had to evacuate to Formosa to escape the Reds, CAT saved a lot of them from death, or worse fates. Anyhoo, a first regatta—or more likely a free-for-all—is planned for this coming Saturday. This fellow Perreira, whose idea the whole thing was, has given a few classes to aspiring captains and deck hands. We'll see if the lessons took.

* * *

This fellow Perreira.

She wouldn't be calling him by his last name for long. You generally don't with a real friend, and to Lily that's what Rocky became. Coletta, too. I can tell you this with confidence, even if I don't know much about the extent or the tenor of those relationships. You never really know much about other peoples' connections, which is something I only figured out after a lifetime of trying to understand the concept of friendship, and mostly from the outside. Lily may have been nervous in Taipei at the start, but she was a social animal. She made friends there. And in Saigon, and everywhere that followed. But Rocky and Coletta became and remained her best friends.

You know what I mean. Best Friends. I know what it means, too, but in the negative. I don't think I've ever truly made one as an adult. Because I've moved around so much. And maybe I've just put too much into protecting myself.

Lily quickly became a deft hostess. I'm talking about her self-confidence. Having Hsiu's help only gave her the space to step into the role and discover how well she could play it. I don't remember parties in Bethesda that were anything like those she began to have in Taipei—26 people for brunch, cocktails for 75, a dinner for 48 seated at six round tables arranged prettily in the walled garden and lit with candles inside red paper globes. They'd been saved from the Lantern Festival, an event where throngs of people paraded through nighttime Taipei's narrow lanes with these beautiful glowing potential incendiary bombs held aloft. At home, in Bethesda I mean, we might have had all of the Neubergs, Rose and Harry, or the Eisensteins, Esther and Sol, with their kids for informal Friday night dinner. Or even several families together for Passover or Thanksgiving, with everybody at long folding tables placed end to end in the living room, and a separate one half a flight down in the family room for the antsy, littlest kids, where somebody older, usually me, was delegated to supervise.

The biggest party that was held at our house in Bethesda was the one for Jordy's bar mitzvah. Lily was a wreck for weeks getting ready, and she was late that evening getting dressed, too. It was ultra-competent Esther whom Lily relied on to make that event happen. *Affair* would be the more accurate word. They always called big, fancy parties affairs. Gramma and Aunt Minna arrived from New York on the Thursday. Gramma commandeered the kitchen to make quarts of chopped liver and hundreds of pieces of strudel. She kept out of the way as Minna naturally tried to take over and boss Lily around. But Esther knew how to manage pushy older women. I don't remember ever meeting her relatives, but surely she had an Aunt Minna corollary, from whom she may have learned how to be pushy herself. In my vague memory, the smoldering and occasional eruptions during preparations for the party took place between

Esther and Minna, with Lily on the sidelines, a placid smile settled on her face.

Lily grew to love being a hostess, and she came to be a renowned one within the USAID circles in Asia. She somehow knew how to seat the right people together to stimulate conversation, how to make introductions that put them at ease, how to generate the sparkle that renders a party memorable. Sid did not contribute much to this, but at least he got out of the way and allowed her to...shine.

I was going to say *flirt*.

She didn't reserve that for the parties she threw. I don't know if it was during that first sailboat outing on Green Lake or one that followed when I saw her and Rocky engaged in what I now recognize to be flirting. Lily reclined on a pile of pillows in the prow of a gondola. Rocky had pulled a wicker chair close. They were facing each other, chatting. They weren't the only people on that boat, but they were focused on each other as if they were alone. That's what I saw. Or, what I thought I saw. I was on another boat bobbing a few yards away, helping Brad Mencken supervise a race between some younger kids. The Junior Scramble, Brad called it, declaring grandly that there would be a silver trophy for the champion.

Jordy was probably the oldest of the youngsters sailing, and he came in first. Then Babby van Kirk, who was second, announced that Jordy's boat had rammed hers at the far end of the course while they tacked for the return run. Thus, Jordy was disqualified. That was the rule. He did not take it well. He hadn't done it *on purpose*, he didn't *know* he had broken a rule—he thereafter went into a vocal and graceless sulk. Maybe he wanted to get Lily's attention, or even get her attention away from Rocky. Or maybe he was really just absorbed with himself, irked by his failure in the moment. Or maybe it was just Jordy asserting to himself—and not for the last time—that life was unfair.

* * *

Midway through the school year, Sid pronounced that the International School wasn't serving Jordy and me well. He argued that the curriculum was too limited, and that most of the teachers weren't trained. "Ignoramuses," he called them, "or, as you would know if they were bothering to teach you Latin, ignorami." It felt a bit as though he were calling Jordy and me stupid. He wasn't wrong about the school's limitations. It was pretty makeshift, as schools go. But his superior attitude was mainly fueled by a disdain for the military—the Army and the Air Force, I mean; those were the branches comprising the American military presence in Taiwan, in his thinking inferior to the Navy. Our teachers were mostly wives of American officers and not necessarily trained to teach. I don't imagine Sid had any problem with the military's mission—after all, he was serving the same government, furthering the same American postwar agenda of global policing in the guise of global benevolence. And in practical and hyperlocal terms, it was the common and, no doubt, correct wisdom that only the presence and size of the U.S. garrison—14,000, I think it was back then—was preventing the Nationalists from being crushed and Taiwan becoming reabsorbed into China.

And Sid is not happy with some of the boys Jordy is going around with. The military boys, the older ones—a lot of Elvis

75

Presley haircuts, if you know what I mean. There just seems to be a very rowdy atmosphere, they're shooting off fireworks all the time and doing God knows what else. Fireworks are cheap as dirt here. The Chinese shoot them off for all occasions. I always think it's gunfire, and jump. That will probably be my lasting memory of the Orient. Anyway, there was an incident where some boys used fireworks to booby-trap one of the pedicabs that wait just outside the school gates to take the children home. The driver was hurt, not seriously, but still. The school did not seem to make an effort to discipline anyone for it.

We went to a PTA meeting recently—a hot one, too. There was a group of interested parents who want to better things—same old story everywhere, I guess. But it was different here because we have military people in the majority—and when a Colonel or General speaks, a Sargent is afraid to argue. It was my first experience of close contact with the so-called military mind, and they sure do take their ranks seriously. I suppose we are spoiled, coming from Bethesda and the Montgomery County schools, but Sid thinks that Jordy and Lauren will find themselves behind when we come home. Even worse, what if we return here for another tour? God forbid. And they complete high school in Taipei and are ill-prepared for college. This is a conversation I dread pursuing—he seems to have already made up his mind, and you know how Sid is.

The alternatives to the International School were few. There were State Department families whose kids were in boarding schools in the States or a few in places like Switzerland and the U.K. At first, Lily balked at the idea that we should be sent away at all, let alone halfway around the world. But Gladys suggested that she look for schools in Hong Kong. Lily had been dying to go to Hong Kong ever since we arrived in Taipei. It was an international free port, so a shopper's dream; anything from anywhere could be had, it was said, and at famously good prices. Then there were the fabled troves of Chinese antiques, and the reported 6,000 tailors ready to run up outfits practically while you waited in their shops.

Perhaps I'm being unfair. Hong Kong surely appealed to Lily because it was big and dense and fascinating and far more cosmopolitan than Taipei—more like New York, where she grew up, or even Washington, sleepy as Washington was in those days. Hong Kong was only 500 miles from Taipei, an easy flight even in that pre-jet era. It was the regional air hub; Sid had changed planes there on his trip to and from Saigon. In fact, American diplomatic family members could travel there for free when space was available on military flights and transport ships. Lily grew interested. And after very efficiently corresponding with several schools there, she was finally enthused about the idea of sending us and coming to visit often. I would just as soon have stayed in Taipei. I had made a few girlfriends—Rosemary Ling, in particular. I was getting very good grades. I was thrilled and delighted, if occasionally repulsed, by Taipei, and I knew that even if I were there for the whole of our two-year tour, I would never be bored by it. This whole thing about being sent away had hurt my feelings.

I don't mean to portray Lily as entirely self-serving here. It's not that the academic argument eluded her. In a letter to Rose, she wrote, *I had a conversation about this with Coletta Simpson, the colored girl at Sid's office who I'm sure I've told you about—she pointed out how both of the kids are so curious and comfortable exploring on their own, even here in this foreign place, and that they will be able to adapt easily enough to another new situation. They both get along with her like a house on fire—I guess she's halfway in age between us and them. She spoke about how important a good educational foundation is. Coletta feels that if she had not graduated from Berkeley High School, which is supposed to be one of the very best public schools in California, she would not have been admitted to the University, no matter how good her grades had been. And then where would she be today? Of course, it's different for her, and anyway she is single and has no children. When I mentioned Coletta's thoughts to my neighbor Gladys, she said it was not her place to offer opinions about our kids. I suppose Gladys, being Southern, doesn't really approve of her, so I will make a point of not bringing them together. I wouldn't want Coletta to feel uncomfortable. It is odd to have a Negro friend. But it's nearly as odd to have a friend from Alabama, too.*

I was touched to read that about Coletta, even if her argument had helped sway the decision in favor of our being sent away to school. Anyway, I didn't regret that after the fact. Still, it hurt my feelings and does so again when I saw that Lily also wrote, *I do wonder if I won't miss them very much. Maybe I feel guilty about sending them away. On the other hand, there are moments when I just think how lovely it will be to have them out of here and not have to bludgeon Jordy awake every morning, or witness him and Sid going at it, or sit through Lauren's breakdowns when she insists that nobody at school likes her. Honestly, sometimes it feels like the adolescent ward of an insane asylum around here— the three of them.*

How easily, it seems, Lily was able to loosen ties, and how offhand when admitting it.

Years later, when I visited Gladys in Georgetown, I asked her about the International School and about families whose kids were sent off to boarding school somewhere else. She said,

"Well, we never considered sending Paul away, but he was just in elementary while we lived in Taipei, so we weren't worried about the school, it seemed fine. He's turned out pretty well, after all—Dean's List. You can't imagine how proud we are. But you know, Lauren, Paul was our only child, and he came into our lives—he was just too precious to us. I couldn't have. It was different."

"Yes, I don't remember being told, but I do remember knowing that story, how he came into your lives. Of course you wouldn't have wanted to—" I almost said, "get rid of him"— "be without him."

"Plus, we'd been to Hong Kong many times, so I could reassure Lily about you two being there. She did say—I think this was just before you went—she did say that she was afraid she'd be very blue without you at home. But Lily! If she ever let things get her down, she sure never showed it to me. She just dove into her work with that orphanage and really began to find her footing. I mean, I liked your mother from the first instant, but I do think people in Taipei were surprised—pleased, I mean—at what a dynamo she turned into. Her committee work, yes—but what a hostess, too. The *best* thing was when she and I would throw a party together. We did that, oh, how many times? Well, I pretty much had to join forces with her, or else lose my own reputation! Oh, I'm kidding. We weren't in competition. It was just—it was just so much fun. Lily is always so much fun. Give her my love."

* * *

79

April 13, 1958

Darling girls,

　As usual, we are all very busy with numerous activities, and the social whirl goes on. It's really a very good life—except for the distance from those I love. I'm afraid Sid is going to insist we return here for a second tour—that's the usual thing, and it will be best for his career. He and the Foreign Service were meant for each other, but such things as my mom and aunt get in the way. I told Sid that Nassau and Bermuda need foreign aid desperately, and that I would be happy to be stationed somewhere like that so I could see everyone a few times a year. We're working on it. Incidentally, they're cooking up another temporary assignment for him in Bangkok, Thailand, next month.

　We narrowed the boarding school search down to one—the only English school in Hong Kong that boards girls also happens to be the only one that is coeducational, so it wasn't much of a decision after all since we really want the kids to be at the same place. It's called St. Botolph's and is run by the Anglican Church. I did mention to the headmaster, with whom I have been corresponding, that we are Jewish, and he explained that about half the students are Chinese and many others are children of diplomats or businessmen from elsewhere living in H.K, so Lauren and Jordy won't be the only oddballs. Anyhow, they are not required to attend the daily chapel. The students wear uniforms, and I'm sure it's stricter and more rigorous than an American public school, and certainly more so than the International School here—where the lax discipline was half the problem in the first place. St. Botolph's seems to be very highly thought of—our friend Rocky Perreira, who grew up in Macau, was actually a boarding student there for a few years, and he's quite brilliant and well-rounded. But he went on to

Yale and then Oxford as a Rhodes Scholar, so we do not know precisely at which institution he came by his worldly smarts. Without my asking, Rocky wrote to the headmaster and sang the kids' praises. We feel very lucky to have made friends with him, I must say. A lovely man.

I've joined a committee that is supporting an orphanage here. The woman who runs it, a Madame Liu, has made it her life's work. It seems that she was married to a very wealthy man who took a concubine and eventually left her. She had been an orphan herself, so she decided to start an orphanage. He left her with money and a large house, but she has put it all into her work and has since sold every possession and reached the end of her resources. She does all this with her own hands along with the help of two old servants who had been with her for years, and whom I suspect she is no longer able to pay. I can't adequately describe the conditions there—she takes in any abandoned child and has some mental cases, polio cases, sickly babies, children with scalps and faces covered with horrible sores. They are so crowded that two big children have to sleep in one tiny bed, which is better than sleeping on the street. They were desperate for whole milk powder and diapers for the babies. Even in these circumstances, as long as they aren't sick with something terrible that's visible, the babies are just darling—all Chinese babies have real fat faces and are gorgeous and irresistible—don't be surprised if I just happen to come home with a few!

* * *

The novel *The Ugly American* was causing a sensation in the diplomatic world that year. It's about American diplomats in an unnamed Asian country and depicts a life of careless luxury in the capital city, not unlike the life people surrounding us had in Taipei. But the title character, whose physical ugliness was meant—with just a *slightly* heavy hand—as irony, was a guy who lived out in the field and invented a cheap bicycle-powered water pump that the poor farmers could use to irrigate their rice paddies. Everyone suspected that it was really a roman à clef of Vietnam, and for a while, the parlor game was trying to identify Foreign Service people here know who might have been models for the book's characters.

Lauren was so enraged by the way some of the people in the book behaved, or else inspired by The Ugly American, that she asked to come with me on one of my visits to the orphanage. Now she has taken it on as her own project. She goes there a few afternoons every week and spends time with the little girls, brushing and braiding their hair and playing little games, and she gets them to teach her songs and sayings in Chinese—it's just heartbreaking to see how quickly they respond to this bit of attention, since they normally get so little. She got a few of her girlfriends to come with her the first time. They all quickly lost interest, but she keeps it up by herself.

Excuse me a minute—I have to adjust my halo. But we aren't only involved in noble enterprises. This week we have three cocktail parties for people who are just arriving or finishing their tours, an official reception at the Ministry of Works (in observance of what, I haven't the foggiest) and a hoedown and barbecue next door at our darling friends the Walters', which is for no other purpose than fun. Gladys invited about 55 people and is having it outdoors. The invitations she made were on brown paper shaped like little moonshine jugs—cute, no?

* * *

I hadn't exactly forgotten that I went with Lily to that orphanage, but I haven't thought about it in years. And it occurs to me that, contrary to Lily's report, it was *her* idea, not mine, that I accompany her. I suspect she thought my presence would amplify her own, extend the impression she wanted to make, being effective, being Lady Bountiful. My second thought was that if I ever had gone back, it must have only been only once or twice. The first thought isn't very charitable, is it? But I do remember feeling used.

Most vividly, I remember the scabs—scabs on the children's arms and legs. And how seeing their scabs made my own skin crawl. I read *The Ugly American* around then. Maybe, as she said, it moved me to action—which resulted in my visiting and perhaps momentarily diverting a few bereft children. Though the book also provided me with something else: the beginnings of a framework for sorting out the torrent of images and feelings stirred up by our looking-glass life in Taipei. Sweltering mornings at the market following behind Hsiu as he barged through the crowds of aggressive haggling shoppers, snotty toddlers, coolies heaving enormous sacks. The ruckus of car horns blaring, oxen lowing, piglets screaming under the knife as spurts of their blood puddled in the dirt. Such mornings, followed within hours by sultry afternoons in the shade of an umbrella, dozing by the pool at the Grand Hotel—we'd joined the hotel's swim and tennis club—palm fronds rustling, waiters silently bearing trays of chicken salad sandwiches with their crusts cut off and frosty tumblers of sweet iced tea.

But why should I feel resentful about the orphanage? I respect the work Lily took on in Taipei, which she went on to pursue everywhere else she lived. And really, what she did was not that different from the work I grew up to do myself. Still, it makes me uncomfortable to see us as somehow the same.

Not fair, is that? To Lily, I mean.

As an adult, I worked mostly in refugee relief. The irony is not lost on me that I found a vocation which mirrored my mother's avocation. The motivations were similar, surely. As well as the gratifications. That kind of work is like sailing. Not the placid sailing we did in Taipei, but like heeling over with sails taut in a filthy storm. You are borne along on a turbulence of pain, empathy, sadness, hope, grit, and occasionally, small success. And you live with guilt over the world's profound inequalities and an awareness of the dependable hull that keeps you slicing through the waves and relatively dry, which is your own good fortune. Speaking of something that's not fair.

Of course, in our day-to-day work, Lily and my situations were dissimilar. I was living in a tent often enough, usually in a field outside some backwater village, and I was a professional. Not like her, living in the villa, in a capital city, a Foreign Service wife asserting a persona while buttressing her husband's career.

Besides, our work affected us so differently. Even to the end, Lily remained buoyant. While describing some group of pitiable children or their bleak prospects, she might genuinely tear up. Yet a few minutes later she would brightly offer drinks or a tidbit of embassy gossip or pull together an expedition to some famous temple or beauty spot. Her need for recognition and her flair for charming it out of people fed her ability to repeatedly face the anguish and frustration of the work. Acclaim replenished her. It is cynical of me to say so, but it's true. And who am I to say that she should have been denied that which allowed her to keep going? She was trying to save lives, not exactly from death, but from impoverished futures. And she succeeded in saving more than a few.

As for me? I didn't seek acclaim. I considered the desire for it to be suspicious, corrupt even. Lily wouldn't have deigned to live in a tent like I did, but she wasn't above maneuvering for praise as a way to keep herself impassioned and rewarded. I suppose I didn't believe in my ability to replicate her kind of life. The clothes, the parties, the poise. I resented her for thinking that I should and expecting that I would. Was that just my way of paying her back for feeling rejected when I had to leave Taipei for school in Hong Kong? A slow-burning, lifelong, teenage tantrum?

Even in her eighties, long-widowed, physically delicate, and easily tired, she was still working to benefit orphans and dining out on her good works and successes. Whereas my passion simply drained away over the years, empathy and idealism paling into numb competence, and finally devolving into exhaustion. I no longer work, no longer confront those heartbreaking scenes, no longer feel that I must find some desperate emollient to offer, or some desperate hope. I was exhausted by it all. I still am.

* * *

The most awful thing happened to poor Lauren yesterday. Our little dog Bomber somehow managed to get out of our garden a few days ago. He's very frisky and probably ran out when somebody had

85

the gate open for a split second too long. By the time we realized he was missing it might have been hours since he'd escaped. It was getting dark, and I confess we didn't look too far for him. It's so chaotic out there, what with the traffic and putrid benjo ditches and lack of streetlights—you don't just go out on foot at night.

But yesterday, Lauren was the only one of us at home when Hsiu came back from the market having recognized one of the men from the squatters' huts at the end of our lane. He was leading Bomber with a string around his neck, apparently trying to sell him at one of the butcher stalls. We hadn't known, but Hsiu informed us with a great deal of Mainlander disdain that this is the time of year called "dog meat season"—evidently, the Taiwanese believe that dog meat is a healthful thing to eat, and that the meat of a black dog like ours is especially so. Lauren very bravely took matters into her owns hands, and she and Hsiu marched down the lane to the little settlement, located the miscreant and confronted him. I can picture Hsiu with his white cook's jacket buttoned to the chin, all puffed up and intimidating over this outrage against his "highest class" American employers, fixing the little man with his withering stare. The dognapper was abashed and led them to a tiny pen in which he had tied up the dog, who was missing his tail, which was apparently already in the soup pot. Lauren says that Hsiu gave the man a real tongue lashing, after which she had Hsiu find her a pedicab and instruct the driver to take her and the dog directly to the veterinary clinic at the university.

I was home by the time she got back with poor, tailless Bomber. His little stump had been painted with gentian violet, and he had received a penicillin shot and a good prognosis. It was only then that Lauren let herself cry like a baby. I felt terrible for her—of course these things happen as we're growing up, awful things we can't avoid witnessing—although this particular tragedy was a new one on me, and honestly, I would laugh if it hadn't been so painful *for Lauren—and for Bomber too. But I was also proud of her for thinking clearly and doing what had to be done. Hsiu cooked Bomber a hamburger, which he gobbled up instantly. He now seems overjoyed to be back inside the gate. I don't worry that he'll run off again any time soon.*

So—file that one under: Mysteries of the East, Strange Culinary Practices.

* * *

It makes me feel a little woozy to read these reports of my teenage meltdowns. Over-emotional reactions have not been a salient feature of the person I became as an adult. Was I so much freer then? Am I so tightly wound now? I might consult a therapist, but surely it's too late for me to change. And I can't see it making any real difference, not to anyone else, alone as I am. And I am well enough used to myself, imperfections included, so why bother?

I certainly think Jordy was in the habit of checking his feelings by the time he became an adult—corking things up and then occasionally letting them explode. Is that how the dynamic works? We had good role models for opacity. An opaque, shiny surface in Lily's case and a surface that didn't even reflect light in Sid's, being that our parents had been greatly absent even when they were present. Or in Lily's case, present but starring in her own show. They were always taking note of who was watching and what any observer might see. And then we kids found ourselves in that buttoned-up, British boarding-school environment, challenged with establishing ourselves once again among strangers just a year after we had to do it in Taipei. Even

Sid's voluble concern about the International School there, which led to our being sent away, did not express itself as warmth toward the two of us. It felt less like concern for the actual Lauren and Jordan Norell than for some pair of generic offspring whose academic futures were just one of many projects he was charged with, and which would reflect on him.

It certainly was Sid who drove that whole decision, although from Lily's narrative you might infer that it was a worry and a process they shared equally. Skepticism about the Taipei school emanated from him. The job of finding another school to ship us off to fell on her. He did stop over in Hong Kong while all that was going on, on his way back to Taipei from his TDY in Bangkok or somewhere, to visit and pass judgement on St. Botolph's. But I don't remember him actually discussing the whole thing directly with me and Jordy.

Our father sailed with us sometimes, but he didn't teach us how to sail. To be fair, he didn't really know how to before we knew Rocky, despite that fact that he'd been in the Navy. I suppose those in Naval Intelligence do not need to know seamanship. Those afternoons sailing at Green Lake or on the Tamsui River were always group events, six or ten families with their kids and their colorful El Toros. I hardly remember a single time when I did something alone with my father. He just wasn't a warm person.

Rocky was warm. Rocky helped get us into St. Botolph's, and he even came to see us there, which Sid never bothered to do. Rocky's visits to the campus always had some other ostensible purpose—he was, after all, an old boy of the school— so he would take tea with the headmaster, or with one of the antiquated fellows who'd taught him 25 years before and was still dozily going at it with our generation. But each time, he would also make a point of finding Jordy and me, which I now see was really the whole point of his being there. Sometimes he would taxi us into the city for an afternoon, and once during a school holiday he took us to Macau to stay in the shadowy, decaying villa inhabited by his elderly aunt, which was also the house where he'd lived out his childhood. There was always something special that Rocky was eager to show us on those visits in Hong Kong. A raucous, signless restaurant that served a bizarre specialty, like snake soup or chicken testicles, or a back-alley shrine misted with incense, or a hidden cove on an uninhabited islet in the estuary, which we would reach on a boat he borrowed from his cousin.

Lily was certainly warmer to us than Sid was—she was a woman, she was our mother, so wouldn't that have been a given? But by the time my parents were working out the school situation, she was already beginning to bask in her emerging persona as hostess and doer of good deeds. She and all the other female members of the international diplomatic community were once invited to an afternoon reception in the august presence of Madame Chiang Kai-Shek. I wasn't there, so I can't say for sure, but I suspect that her contact with the great lady was limited to a few seconds, nothing more than shaking hands in a receiving line. Lily, when retelling the story afterwards, allowed that they had shared an intimate conversation during which the Generalissimo's wife expressly thanked her for all her work in support of that orphanage. Lily beamed while telling it. And during every retelling.

* * *

I don't know if the message that our friend Rocky wrote to the headmaster helped, but we have received a very gracious letter saying that there is definitely room for the kids at St. Botolph's, and that they are expected on Sept. 1—only six weeks from now. We really feel this is the best action in the long run. Jordy doesn't know that they were accepted yet—he and his buddy, Tommy, are on a jaunt around Taiwan, hitching rides on Civil Air Transport planes. CAT only flies small planes on their routes within the island, as well as a couple of C-47s left over from the war, which don't have regular seats, just benches along the sides. The boys were on one of those when they left from Taipei—we saw them aboard— Jordy was so thrilled. Into the wild blue yonder.

* * *

Before we left for Hong Kong, Lily and Sid took us for a weekend up to Sun Moon Lake, a resort high in the mountains of central Taiwan. Like nearly every other beautiful place on Earth, it's been developed to death since then, but at the time there were only a scattering of private villas on the steep, forested slopes above the shore, and a couple of inns and government guest houses, one of which we stayed in. The lake is at the center of the traditional homeland of an aboriginal tribe. There was a little tourist installation, a shack of a museum and an area of beaten earth where women with tattooed faces and supposedly traditional costumes did a little circle dance for us. We were the only spectators present at that moment. It was embarrassing. The scenery was beautiful, but Jordy and I were bored out of our minds. We would have preferred to have had a few more days to run around Taipei.

Jordy and I had quickly grown comfortable setting off to explore on our own or with friends—though we mostly did so separately. It had not taken long after the initial shock for the ever-present poverty to lose its novelty, nor for us to take for granted the opulence and freedom of our own situation. Taiwan was poor then, most people's lives were hard, but I don't think anybody was starving. You didn't see beggars in the streets. Taiwan felt wide open to us, which it was, even though we were just kids. Nowhere seemed off limits. We felt no sense of menace. Of course, we didn't realize that the island was governed as a police state. The very visible U.S. military presence, though meant for protection from the Mainland Communists, can only have reinforced this reality in the popular consciousness. Anybody who bothered American Foreign Service brats would have been asking for trouble.

I've since spent time in far poorer, more desperate, and more dysfunctional places than Taiwan was in the late Fifties— Bangladesh, Cambodia after the fall of the Khmer Rouge—and learned that coming to terms with the contradiction of other people's impoverishment and your own relative wealth is a requisite for psychic survival. You can't solve the problem of the family making their home from a cardboard carton on the sidewalk outside your hotel. And you can't let it paralyze you or provoke you to terrorism, either. That's not to say there shouldn't be an attempt to solve these problems, or that you shouldn't participate in trying. I've tried. I could even say I've sacrificed in trying.

Were she here today, Lily would not hesitate to point out that, had I followed her lead—taken the path she fancied and that she and my father were clearing for Jordy and me—I could be living in a lavish house with a walk-in closet full of pretty

91

outfits and a maid, and I could proceed to bejewel my golden years with tours to all of the fascinating corners of the globe I've never seen. Instead, I'm perched in this high-rise studio apartment with its view of the freeway, making occasional excursions on foot to the public library and city park. But I'm sick of travel. I've been fascinated to the point of exhaustion by the globe. Yes, I could have ended up wealthier. I have Social Security and Medicare, a bit of savings and whatever remains from what Lily left when she died. I have my balcony, with its slightly distracting views of the urban bustle and its protective vertical distance above all that. I'm not insecure.

In Lily's computation of my current hardship, she would have included my lack of a husband and family. As if her own had been such a sterling success. I suppose I don't know what I'm missing there. But while my modest finances might be accurately judged as a function of my career choices, it would be a mighty stretch to blame my solitude on them. It's probably the other way around: I made a rootless life working here and there across Asia as a way to remain alone. Still, regarding wealth, we're all trapped by circumstance, flotsam on the tides of history. Lily would call me poor as I am now. The family living in the cardboard box would know with certainty that I am rich.

What about my hysterics after our dog was snatched, early in our time in Taipei? That was certainly a conflicted encounter between poverty and privilege. It was both the pain of my puppy that I was reacting to, and the unpleasant revelation that the people living in the lean-tos down the lane were reduced to making soup out of captured pets. By then I was already learning to defend myself from the pain that history inflicts on masses of people. People whose names you never know. Of course, I have been affected by the individuals, the ones I've met, who looked into my eyes, or didn't, when telling their individual stories. Though, even then—well, you have to protect yourself. Grow a skin or leave your nerves exposed.

Jordy and I had become comfortable in Taipei. Now, so soon, we were being sent to a different foreign place. Coming from sleepy Taipei, Hong Kong had the glittery allure of a metropolis, an entrepot, the cosmopolitan hub which it was and still tenuously remains—I pictured it accurately even before seeing it: a buzzing place crowded with people and ships and planes racing in every direction, and labyrinthine, with something startling down every alleyway. The school was a completely different, insulated environment, both physically and culturally. Its neat campus of spacious lawns and playing fields was well outside the urbanized area. The red brick buildings, though neither particularly old nor swathed in ivy, looked like they'd been lifted from some venerable English public school. As did the uniforms.

There were shops in Hong Kong that specialized in these garments, made in the traditional flannels and tartan wools, plus new-fangled, hot-season versions in Terylene, which is what the English called polyester. That stuff allowed the creases in our plaid skirts to be knife-edged and permanent. The material was supposed to be cooler. Sweat did dry off it fairly fast. I liked St. Botolph's well enough, but I was never comfortable in those unforgiving clothes. Lily would have preferred having them tailored for us in Taipei, but it wasn't possible to get the material. Besides, those pleats must have been permanently pressed at the factory where they made the fabric. The day we went to St. Botolph's, we were met at the airport by a school matron who took us directly to buy our first uniforms. This made the transition doubly disorienting—all "Come along now," no chance to let our gaze linger on anything, never mind actually poking around in this new place. Suddenly, we were in a taxi, and then we were in the shop, then in a taxi again, and then suddenly we were at school.

Jordy and I did get to know Hong Kong a bit, although we never felt as comfortable there as we had in Taipei. It was such a bigger, more complicated and, I suppose, scarier place. Although I wasn't aware of being afraid while I was there. The rough ways of life that had scared me in Taipei didn't exist in Hong Kong. I mean, of course they existed—impoverished squatters, exploding coal-fired water heaters, visible diseases— but they weren't visible to me. They were in places we never went to, or they were disguised or blocked from our view by Hong Kong's dense bustle and relative prosperity. It also took us a while to get to know Hong Kong at all because there was so much more to it, and we were only able to see the city in fragments on days when there were school trips, or when we were allowed to venture forth on our own. Such as when we stayed there through the school holidays, since it wasn't convenient for our parents to have us return to Taipei. Or when we were permitted to leave campus for the day because Lily was visiting. Or Rocky. Or both.

I spent a farewell afternoon with Rosemary before we left for St. Botolph's, sunning by the pool, at the Grand. Her mother had never let her come with Lily and me to the orphanage. They considered it to be beneath their aristocratic station. "But I admire *your* mother so much," Rosemary said, lifting her modish cat eye sunglasses for emphasis. Rosemary was fashion conscious, so I wasn't certain whether it was Lily's style or her good works that she was talking about. But

Rosemary said something similar when I saw her years later. "It was knowing what your mother tried to do for those children that first made me consider becoming a doctor." Along with all the bereft and abandoned kids Lily had impacted over the years, she had changed the life of at least one young patrician, too.

* * *

Jordy and Lauren leave this Friday afternoon for Hong Kong, and I must say there are a few moments when I wonder if we are making a mistake in sending them away. Hong Kong may look close to Taiwan from the distance of Washington, but it's still another country and across the water, and we can't expect to see them all that often. Sid is being sent to Vientiane in a month or two for a few weeks' temporary duty, and since you have to change planes in Hong Kong, he might try to visit them. I'm hoping I might get to Hong Kong myself before long.

Well, I've finally had a tangle with a pedicab. The traffic here looks simply impossible—but somehow it seems to sort itself out in front of you when you are driving. You keep your foot on the brake and a heavy hand on the horn. Actually, blowing the horn does not mean that anyone will move out of your way. It just tells the pedestrian or cyclist or buffalo cart driver that you have seen them, and they are not to worry, and you wish them a good day! So, this pedicab driver swerved out, or I swerved in, and his wheel and my fender got rather involved. His English being nil and my Chinese not for him, we didn't get very far. I handed him my address and phone number and went on my way. A couple of hours later, both he and the Foreign Affairs Police appeared at our gate. However,

*our insurance company paid him at once for a new wheel and fixed
our fender. Thus, peace between nations reigns again.*

* * *

I eventually settled in at St. Botolph's, made friends, and did
well. For Jordy, it was a different story. He resented the
regimentation, which kept him from hopping on his bike and
exploring at will as he had in Taipei. That half-smile of his was
put to use more frequently as a weapon of passive-aggression.
He got into trouble a lot. Why didn't we see where Jordy was
headed? I mean, why didn't my parents see it? It was their job,
not mine.

I did know something wasn't right. He was a couple years
behind me. We had different circles of friends. But kids have
eyes, and kids talk. I could see which boys he was running with
at the International School in Taipei. They were the kind who
used to be called "hards"—an out-of-date term for greasers and
punks. Bad boys. Lily, rather self-servingly, dismissed them as
military brats in her letters, implying that it was just a matter of
class, lower-class or military-class. Thus neatly evading the
possibility that Jordy was responsible for anything those kids
did, or for his own behavior. As if no "highest class" Foreign
Service kids or children of American businessmen making
fortunes under the protection of the U.S. and its military
enforcers could possibly be bullies. Or bullied.

The worst of the hards in Taipei was Andy Everett, son of
the American president of the Taiwan subsidiary of an
American shipbuilding company. His father was about as much
of a plutocrat as anybody we knew in Taipei. There was an

incident I didn't witness when an American kid forced a pedicab off the road into a canal. Maybe the rumors garbled it, but supposedly while it was Andy's idea, it was Jordy who—taking the dare?—stepped into the driver's path, forcing him to choose between colliding with an American and thereby suffering a likely encounter with the police, or steering off into the sludge. So I knew the reputation Jordy was acquiring. He wasn't a leader, but was easily led. I feebly tried talking to him about it once, not that I knew how to go about it. "You don't have to do everything those guys tell you," I said. "What's so great about them anyway? There are nicer kids in your class. What about Rosemary's brother, Edmund?"

"Ugh. Edmund Ling is a drip," Jordy snapped. "You don't know anything about it, Laur. Just leave me alone."

Sid and Lily recognized the problem. But they saw it as an effect of being in the school environment in Taipei, not that it was something within their son. It was a key factor in why they sent us off to Hong Kong. To them, the problem was solved. As in, removed from sight. My parents seemed to think that the structure of a British-model boarding school was a solution. If you were an engaged student at St. Botolph's, showed interest in the curriculum, asked intelligent questions, did the work, you might attract some attention and support from the faculty. If you were a smoldering, good-looking boy, you might attract a different kind of attention—I don't know what rumors were true. But as I said, kids talk. And it was on the model of the British public school—you know what they say about those. I don't know if anybody was coercing Jordy to have sex, for example. I do know for certain that the school wasn't offering any kind of therapy. The concepts of "guidance counselor" or "therapist" were far too newfangled, or maybe too American, for St. Botolph's, and there weren't any.

After St. Botolph's, Jordy went back to Maryland, to the university, and found himself alone among many thousands of freshmen. It couldn't have been easy. He may have known a handful of kids from Bethesda from half a dozen years earlier, but my impression is that if he was able to find them, he didn't connect with any of them. I know that Esther and Rose and other friends of Lily's would invite him to come to their homes for the High Holidays and Thanksgiving, but I guess he didn't see our family friends as having anything to do with him. Rose told me, when I saw her some years after that—before she descended into senility, on that same trip to Washington when I visited Gladys in Georgetown—that he came to stay with her once or twice, and that she and Harry and Margo, their daughter, then had a date to pick him up in College Park one Sunday and go to lunch, but he stood them up. "I was sick about it," Rose said. "I left messages at his dorm, but never heard from him again. I felt responsible. I knew something was wrong, but—well! I did know *something* was wrong. Because this was after Lily and Sid came on home leave and had snubbed us already."

I had a similar experience at Michigan, arriving without even a few acquaintances, but I was better than Jordy at making friends back then. And unlike Jordy, I did not promptly flunk out. Later, he turned up again in Taipei after Lily and Sid had moved on—they were in Saigon by then. I suppose Lily liked to think that Rocky, who was still in Taipei, was attending to Jordy. I don't doubt that Rocky liked Jordy. He did help him out. I can't say whether Rocky had any skills at parenting, or mentoring, or at being anything more than superficially avuncular. I doubt he saw his role that way, or even consciously considered that he had a role. Jordy was just his good friend's kid, a kid he probably liked but who was not his responsibility.

* * *

Well, the kids are gone, and Sid is in Laos until early next month, so I am feeling a bit at loose ends. Plus, now there's this little ol' ruckus that the Communists are kicking up by shelling them thar offshore islands. It began just when Jordy and Lauren left for Hong Kong. It gave me quite a scare, but I think they must be safer there than we may be here. It's the unofficial topic of the day at all the parties. Any comments in the papers in Wash.? Those islands are in the Nationalist's hands, even though they are something like 100 miles from Taiwan, within spitting distance from the Mainland coast. Why they're called "offshore" is beyond me—they're not exactly off this shore. Anyway, the Red Chinese beef is with the Nationalists and with the U.S. because we back them, but not really with the British, who have Hong Kong. As our friend Rocky explained to me, the Reds need Hong Kong just as it is, since it provides them with a gateway to move things in and out of Mainland China. Black market goods. And spies, I suppose he meant. We must have a few spies here among us in Taipei, too. But that is certainly not something that is openly speculated upon.

So Rocky put my mind at ease, as far as the kids' situation at school goes. He also took pity on me in my solitary state and invited me out on his boat on Labor Day, along with several others. It was an extremely hot day with hardly any wind, and after an hour or so he could see that everyone was getting grumpy. So he made the brilliant suggestion that we abandon ship (Not literally—we motored back to the dock.) and regroup by the pool at the Grand Hotel, with a promise to take everybody sailing again in cooler weather. Of course, it being an office holiday for all the Americans, the Grand was mobbed, but we found a spot under an umbrella and sipped icy drinks and ended up passing a charming afternoon, which cheered me up considerably.

* * *

I must have become so quickly immersed in school life, or else the school kept us so protected from events outside its walls, that I wasn't even aware of those islands being shelled while it was happening. Years later, when I saw Esther Eisenstein in Bethesda—the day she first told me about the scrapbook of Lily's letters—she mentioned several times how frightened all our friends back home had been. "We thought it was the beginning of World War III," she said. I suggested that attitude must have been so prominent because they were in Washington, where international conflicts always loomed so large. "No darling, it was because we were worried about *you*, because you were people we knew, and we thought you were in danger," Esther said. "We had lived through the war, you know. Some of us had relatives in Europe who—you know. But your mother—I don't understand how she managed to dismiss it so easily. All those cocktail hours and new friends, I suppose. Boating parties."

* * *

Plans have been drawn up for all of us dependents to be evacuated to a base in Japan at a moment's notice. Should it happen, I shall spend the flight drawing up a shopping list and head to Takashimaya the moment we land in Tokyo. The Embassy also decided to install bomb shelters at all of our houses—and thus ensued the elaborate process. It took three days of a dozen workmen appearing to instruct each other in how to dig a big hole in our garden, into which they sunk what appears to be a length of—new and perfectly clean—concrete sewer pipe. It has a hinged metal lid and metal rungs you would climb down after pulling the lid shut behind you. There are some metal seats that fold down from the sides. It's been in place for about two weeks, during which time (according to my cook, Hsiu, who peeked in this morning) it has accumulated a few inches of rainwater and a resident snake. God forbid the Red Chinese planes should come. I'll just crawl under the bed. But they have not shot off anything new in the direction of the offshore islands for the last few days, so the feeling here is that the whole set-to may have died down.

There was one real scare when, in the middle of all this, our friend Rocky Perreira set off in his sailboat for the Pescadores— that's a little group of nearby islands belonging to Formosa that are supposed to be simply gorgeous and unspoiled with the most beautiful beaches—but since there are no decent hotels, nobody goes there. He is a very experienced sailor, so we didn't think anything of him making the trip on his own, until he didn't return as promised. It transpired that a fierce storm blew up just as he was approaching the harbor, which rammed him into a reef. He had to swim ashore—the boat was a total loss, and he lost all his money and passport, too. He had quite a time explaining himself to the officials there, who I imagine must be rather jumpy at the moment—the Pescadores are closer to Formosa than the islands that were shelled lately, but they do lie in that general direction. Anyhoo,

Rocky leads a charmed life and is now dining out all over town on this swashbuckling tale. And he has already been down to the boatyard to commission a replacement for the shipwreck.

What's the local gossip? I absolutely feel as if you are all in another world that I once vaguely knew. You grow very involved with a foreign place when you live there. You want to know more about it than just the surface details that made the first impressions. I had a most fascinating conversation at dinner the other night with a professor of Chinese history. His family were of high rank in the court of this dynasty or that for centuries and centuries—he is now at Johns Hopkins and was back here to visit his parents. However, many of his relatives never escaped the Mainland and some have actually been executed by the Communists. I couldn't help thinking of Germany and Poland and people who didn't escape in time. He explained some old customs, such as foot-binding. It was only ever practiced by the upper-classes—a woman shouldn't be able to leave, of course—but she also shouldn't be able to do any work, since work would be beneath her station in life and cause her husband to lose face. It was outlawed after Sun Yat-sen modernized things. But even here and in this day, you still might see an elderly lady hobbling along in the tiniest little shoes. Simply painful and awful to watch. The shoes themselves are beautiful tho, in different colored brocade silk, like little pieces of upholstered doll furniture. You can hold a pair in your palm, they're that tiny. I have bought a few antique ones—they make a pretty arrangement.

Sid will be going off on another temporary assignment the week after next. With him gone and the kids too, I realized that I just can't spend Thanksgiving here alone—of course I will have all manner of gracious invitations to dinner on the day, but I've always felt that Thanksgiving is a holiday for being together with one's family and closest friends—you will understand what I mean. And

I would miss you old friends terribly if I were to spend the day with new ones. So, I have decided to visit Hong Kong.

This will be my first trip off the island since we arrived in Taiwan. H.K. is a much more sophisticated city than Taipei by all accounts, so I'm very excited. I won't have any Thanksgiving dinner there, either, but I'll be able to see the kids when they're not in class or pursuing other school activities. I already have the name of a highly recommended tailor and will have some things made. They work very fast—I understand you can get a suit fitted and finished overnight—they must never sleep. And there are wonderful fabrics available. Please send me pictures of cocktail dresses from the magazines posthaste—I need to have one or two made up, but I don't have any inspiration as to style. And I haven't the vaguest what <u>they</u> are wearing this year.

* * *

I was wrong previously. There was one other letter that Lily wrote by hand, the one on pages and pages of purloined hotel stationery that she scrawled while she was in the Hong Kong airport waiting for her flight back to Taipei. It's mostly written in her usual, vivid travelogue mode—fascinated, charmed, evocative, and intense like the city she describes. *Wherever you find yourself, there's almost always a view of the harbor, which is busy and crammed with ships and boats of every description from every corner of the world. You're constantly hopping on and off ferries to get to the other side.* Coletta, who had been to Hong Kong before and could speak Chinese, had taken a few days' leave to accompany Lily and serve as guide. They arrived on a

Friday, so Jordy and I were able to spend the weekend with them.

We took in all of the main sights, like Tiger Balm Gardens, which is a mountainside park filled with fantastic bridges and pagodas and stone lions, built by a family who got rich off selling a camphor ointment—the Oriental Ben Gay. We rode the Peak Tram, a cable car that goes up almost vertically to the top of a mountain—I really had to look at my shoes to keep from becoming sick, but once you catch your breath you have a simply stunning view of everything, with the boats crossing back and forth. And Coletta knew to take us for dinner to a most picturesque area of the harbor, where hundreds of sampans are lashed together like a floating island, each boat being a family's actual home and also their means to a living earned by fishing or from hauling trash or whatever they specifically do.

Coletta went back to Taipei that Monday. Lily came out to school, had tea with the headmaster, met a few of our teachers and approved highly of everything she saw. *Jordy has jumped into sports, but of course they are different games—he's learning rugby and cricket. He had a black eye and a cut on his cheek, which of course concerned me but evidently it was just an accident that happened while playing rugby—such a rough game.* Then Lily was on her own for a few days. She visited a tailor and ordered a bunch of clothes—the description makes it sound like an entirely new wardrobe. *I suppose I went a little crazy, but I am schlepping it all back to Taipei for the grand total of $102— which includes the price of an extra suitcase to hold it—and it was all completed in less than a week! I did have to go a second time for a fitting. I also spent one afternoon at a most interesting museum of Chinese art and archeology. And then, just as I was starting to get a little bored, what should happen but our friend Rocky Perreira* showed up at my hotel on Wednesday nite. The Embassy offices in Taipei were closing for the long Thanksgiving weekend. He has no family there, so he decided to visit Macau, which is where he grew up and still has relatives. And he talked me into going with him.

Thursday morning, Rocky and I caught the ferry—the distance to Macau is only 40 miles, but the ride takes four hours. You slowly pass by dozens of islands. Some of them are just big rocks jutting out of the sea, which is plied in every direction by sampans, junks, speedboats, and freighters large and small. Close to Hong Kong, we saw very trim patrol boats belonging to the British Royal Navy—there were also a few of our U.S. 7th Fleet in port, which R. and I crisply saluted, to the great amusement of the other passengers, who were mainly Chinese (or Macanese, as they are called if they live in Macau). Then we docked at Macau next to a single, decrepit relic of a Portuguese war ship. Left over from God alone knows which war.

We stayed with Rocky's great aunt—his grandfather's sister, who is 87 and widowed, but still lives in the old family home. It is in a lovely, quieter section of very large houses, itself being very spacious and filled with antique furniture, mostly Chinese. The floors and walls in the halls and stairways are all done in blue and white tiles that were brought from Portugal as ballast in trading ships ages ago. The aunt, Benedita, speaks English fairly well, and from talking with her, I finally have a better grasp on Rocky's background. Whenever you try to ask him, he just smiles and says it's too complicated. Their ancestor came as a merchant to Macau almost two hundred years ago and established this line of the family. Apparently, very few of them ever went back to Portugal—well it was quite a journey in the days before steamships. They just sent back for girls to marry.

Anyhow, Rocky's father went to medical school in the U.S., where he married an American and Rocky was born, which gives Rocky dual citizenship. They returned to Macau when he was quite small, but then the mother died of TB. So this Aunt Benedita was like a second mother to him as he was growing up—he and his father lived with her in that house. Because of his U.S. citizenship, they wanted him to be fluent in English, so that's why he went to school at St. Botolph's in Hong Kong. Then he attended college at Yale and went on to graduate school at Oxford. All of this accounts for his accent, which you have a hard time putting your finger on but is so debonair and charming, like Cary Grant's. The father died just a few years ago—heart attack.

We had such a fascinating time walking through old streets with heavenly names: Rua da Felicidade—Street of Happiness— and Patio da Ilusao—Courtyard of Illusion. Did you ever? And enjoyed a long, tipsy outdoor lunch with Portuguese "green wine" at a restaurant terrace overlooking the harbor—utterly divine and everything enchanting. I'm feeling so full and, honestly, drained at the same time. Can't wait to get on the plane and sleep my way back to Taipei.

Love,
Lily

* * *

I don't know exactly what response that drew from her friends at home, but the following letter in the scrapbook included this:

I must say I was surprised at your comments re my recent trip to HK. I guess it's hard to realize from such a distance, and since you have never been in this part of the world yourself, but it is perfectly safe to travel in a place like Hong Kong, even as a woman on her own. People just do not cause trouble with Americans, but are simply gracious and considerate. Anyway, I was hardly alone, as you know, between Coletta and Rocky.

Yes, it is unusual to have a Negro friend—I certainly never have had one before. I think the most contact people like you and I have ever really had with them has been with our maids, with whom we do not of course go out to dinner or anything like that. But Coletta is an educated and very well-spoken girl. And somehow differences just seem to matter less in this environment. You are always meeting and socializing with people from the most unusual backgrounds. I was seated at a dinner recently next to, of all people, the Egyptian Ambassador—utterly charming and sophisticated, and perfectly fluent in veddy British English, don'tcha know—we scrupulously did <u>not</u> discuss religion or Israel and the Arabs.

This sort of thing is normal to us now, odd as it may sound. And you know, we have encountered hardly any anti-Semitism here, other than an occasional offhand remark from one or two of the U.S. Embassy people, who are of the Ivy League or D.A.R. type, and what can you do? But not from the Chinese or anybody else we have met. Now that I think about it, I realize what a relief it is— you stop wondering whether people you are pleasantly talking to might actually have some very different thoughts about you all because they know your background—instead you can just concern yourself with whether your slip is showing. And honestly! Rocky Perreira is a perfect gentleman. You have <u>absolutely</u> <u>nothing</u> to worry about on that score.

* * *

That perfect gentleman took Jordy and me to Macau once during a school holiday. He left us there for a week or two with only his elderly aunt and her amah. I remember that house being less enchanting than how Lily described it—interesting for its history and architecture but shadowy, dusty, and unnervingly quiet. Cloistered. So Jordy and I got a taste of yet another Chinese city, another variation on the theme of the Chinese city. Most days, we took long walks together around the harbor, through back alleys, into markets and shops. Between us, we knew enough of the language to get around easily. We loved the street food. And we didn't have anything better to do.

That trip to Macau was actually when my fear of the world dissolved. I can't explain it, but somehow I knew at the time that it was happening. Although, there was nothing horrible or bizarre that I had to confront while we were there. I can't remember any cathartic moment. Still, there was a change I perceived within myself, a sort of dawning. Maybe it was because Macau felt both strange and familiar, but was so much calmer than Hong Kong? And there were no demands on us. We were free for those few days. Like my parents and my brother, I ended up spending most of my life in Asia. And much of that was spent in pretty challenging situations. But after that trip, nothing Asia ever again threw at me made me recoil or dissolve. I can't say I fully understand this, but I've appreciated it more times than I can count.

I just recalled that Lily and everybody else sometimes referred to Rocky as a confirmed bachelor. Wasn't that, in those days, a euphemism for being gay? Rocky, I'm almost certain, was not gay. I can imagine that he could render any gay man weak in the knees, since he had that effect on women. I suppose if you thought he was gay it would appear as if Lily was his beard. She may have been his lover or may only have been his friend, but I believe whatever they had was genuine. And a cynical observer might have suspected that Rocky only took an interest in Jordy and me to get near her. But it occurs to me now, thinking about the empty feeling of that big, lifeless house in Macau and Rocky having been an only child—and myself now, childless and single—that maybe it was only that he longed for a family of his own, and ours was a kind of surrogate.

Besides, he liked us, and we liked him. We definitely wished he had stayed with us in Macau that time, instead of parking us with Aunt Benedita. We wouldn't have had to manufacture our own diversions, that's for sure.

* * *

Our kids have been home for the past week, and of course it is wonderful to have them here. They have been enjoying parties and outings with the teenage set, gone sailing a couple of times, as well as having accompanied us to various grown-up Xmas festivities. Jordy and some boys are leaving tomorrow to go hiking in the mountains, where they will stay for several nites in a Buddhist hostel at a hot spring. Don't worry, he doesn't intend to convert. But I was pleased to learn that he has become fascinated by Chinese history from a course taught at the school. It's the first subject that seems to have really captured his interest, academically, although he still loves to tinker with machinery. I was touched that he spent a long time in the kitchen the other day asking Hsiu and Wei about their families' backgrounds and their experiences on the Mainland and the terrible situation for the people there under the Reds.

Afterwards, Hsiu said to me that he believed Jordy would grow up to be a true friend of the Chinese people, and honestly, he was on the verge of tears when he said it. I wish you could know what a sweet fellow he is.

* * *

I, of course, wasn't involved in my parents' decision to accept a second tour in Taipei. For all I know, it took them five minutes to discuss. It's clear they both wanted it. But Lily seems to have soft-pedaled the news to her friends back home. She scattered hints over several months of correspondence. In January, she wrote, *I will be no fun at all when we return—you will only hear me whining at the loss of my delightful servants. And missing my orphans, too. They are so darling and sad and need me so much.* Then, a few weeks later: *I feel that I'm making a real contribution, which is so gratifying. And I guess I am afraid I will find the normalcy of life back home a bit dull.* And a subsequent letter contained this passage that implies quite the opposite of what was already planned: *I already feel nostalgic. The other day I walked over to a friend's to attend a committee meeting—about four blocks away through some muddy, smelly lanes with all the normal signs of poverty and life on display—and I suddenly couldn't even remember what a street in the U.S. looked like. I am seeing everything with renewed interest, in case these will be my last impressions.* Could she have been so duplicitous? Do I have the chronology confused? Was it a Freudian slip, and she meant to say, "in case these *would have been* my last impressions if we weren't coming back here after home leave?" Jordy and I were made use of in this disinformation campaign, too: *It seems not*

110

such a good idea to yank them out of there for yet another school—three changes in as many years. I just don't think that's a good idea, do you?

In April, she finally made it clear, but immediately attempted to soften the news in the following paragraph.

We will just have to talk like crazy and catch up while we're there on home leave. Also, now that the airlines are starting to fly the new jet planes, the idea of you guys visiting us here is not so outlandish. They don't come to Taipei yet, but Japan Air Lines is already using the jets between San Francisco and Tokyo, which is practically around the corner. This is an aviation fact that I have learned from Jordy, who is crazy for anything that flies. He calls the DC-8 "the airliner of tomorrow." Does my boy have a future in the airline industry, or perhaps in advertising? Anyway, with the kids in Hong Kong most of the time, we have plenty of room for guests. I promise to wine and dine all who make the trek—that will be rice wine, natch, and I shall require you to use chopsticks, so start practicing now—and then you will see for yourselves how gorgeous this life really is.

But what exactly was the news she meant to soften? That she and her friends would unfortunately be separated for at least another two years? Or that she was leaving them behind for good?

* * *

Fill your percolators and set out the cups, began a letter Lily wrote in May that detailed the home leave travel plans. Home leaves were normally two months long. In Washington, the State Department would put us up in a hotel downtown, since there were tenants in our Bethesda house. But we'd have a rental car, so she assured her friends that seeing them in the suburbs would be easy. Because of our British school calendar, which didn't include an American-style long summer vacation, Jordy and I would only be in Washington for three weeks. Then we were to fly back to Hong Kong on our own. *Such seasoned travelers now, they'll be fine.* But Sid and Lily would only be there a few days longer. They were going to make a month's grand tour, returning to Taiwan traveling east, not west. They would sail on the *Queen Elizabeth* from New York to Southampton, and then travel via Paris, Venice, Athens, Tel Aviv, and Delhi, with a side trip from there to Agra to see the Taj Mahal.

The glamour of these arrangements must have induced a twinge of guilt in advance. Evidently, Lily had taken the little Olivetti with her to the Grand Hotel the day she wrote that letter, because she goes on to say, *I am lolling on my rear by the pool—and were it not for the sprinkling of Chinese faces among the members, and the Chinese waiters, and the terraced mountains in the background, I could well imagine that I were in the U.S.A. It is very easy here to grow blind and deaf to the dirt, the poverty and the endless labor with which the great mass of the population lives. Unfortunately, it is true that many of the Americans here do nothing but lead lives of complete ease and luxury. But then, that is true even at home. Of course, we ourselves never had it so good, but at least we've never gotten used to the contrast. Sid in his work, and I in my small way, are trying to help however we can.*

I don't know exactly what brought this all on—except that while driving over here, I passed a man bent double, pulling a cart laden with an unbelievable load of scrap iron—you can't imagine the feeling, seeing a man doing the work of a beast, but it's such a common sight. However, my car broke down as I was coming up the hill to the hotel—so I felt a little sorry for me, too.

* * *

Returning to Washington for home leave, we kids flew from Hong Kong to Tokyo, where we met up with Sid and Lily before flying on to Honolulu, San Francisco, and D.C. Our flight from Hong Kong was on a British Overseas Airways Corporation de Havilland Comet. The Comet was actually the world's first commercial jet airliner, and this was our first experience flying on a jet. Jordy, you will not be surprised to hear, was elated. We both marveled at how much smoother and quieter the ride seemed. You have probably never heard of, let alone flown in, a de Havilland Comet. The model did not remain in service for very long. It had an unfortunate tendency to break apart and fall from the sky.

2.

They returned for another tour. Surely, she must have continued writing home, even if the letters were less frequent as life overseas became quotidian and her ties to Washington more attenuated. Or maybe she didn't. In any case, no more letters were saved. "The idea all along had been that your family was going overseas for just two years," Esther Eisenstein told me when I saw her in 2008, a hint of exasperation in her tone even after all that time. Lily had just died. I was 66 and ready to stop. I didn't want to care any longer—or couldn't find the energy— to try to save people or help them save themselves, whichever it was. I was also stunned at finding myself to be an orphan—my father was gone by then, too.

I went back to Washington to settle some legal matters and spent an afternoon with Esther. She was packing to move out of the house she had lived in for more than half a century. "We all thought it was just going to be a two-year thing, and then be over. Lily had thought so, too. And we were so thrilled by how she described it, she made us feel as if we were there with her. Of course, once she and Sid decided to make the Foreign Service their life…well." Esther gave a little shrug of irritation. "It made me wonder why we bothered saving the letters. There certainly didn't seem any point in keeping it up after that. Did she even write to us anymore? I really can't remember."

Then why did Esther still have the letters? Hadn't the point been to return them to Lily? "Oh." Esther shrugged again. "If you ask me, she deliberately forgot to take them."

She softened as memories welled up. "We had such a marvelous circle of friends then—Sol and I and your parents, Rose and Harry, Clara and poor Louis Cantor, who was the first of our friends to ever die, Jeanette and Irv, the Fonorows, the Kleinwalds—you remember all these people, don't you, darling?"

"Esther, it's been so long. I hate to say it, but they're mostly just names to me now. You and Rose—of course, that's different."

"They're mostly gone now, anyway," she said, with another shrug. "Well! We were so young. We were all couples involved in founding the temple, the very first synagogue in Montgomery County, you know. You could find a nice house out here—construction had started up again after the war—we could buy new cars again. We all had young families, and there wasn't a better place in the world to bring up a family. Most of our husbands worked in the District, but in those days, you could drive downtown from here in 25 minutes, or take the streetcar from Friendship Heights. Sol was still at Commerce. I used to drop him off most days at the streetcar. You must remember that Buick convertible I had—white with the red leather upholstery? You kids were always begging me, 'Aunt Esther, put the top down!'"

"Your white convertible. Of course I remember that—riding with you. I used to love it. I haven't thought of it in…I don't know how long."

"That car was like something from Hollywood." She beamed. "But heavy, like a cast-iron bathtub. The car we had after the Buick came with power steering, and I thought, 'My God, how on Earth did I find the strength?' Back then, we were like pioneers out here. That must sound strange because it was a perfectly lovely place, but there were still neighborhoods that were restricted. You know. No Jews."

"And no Black people, either. Of course."

Esther sped past that. "And you have no idea how sharing such an effort, founding a synagogue, brings people together. From scratch, we did everything—establish a board, recruit members, raise money, hire a rabbi, buy the land, put up the building, set up the Hebrew school and the nursery school. And didn't we run a summer day camp too in the early years? It wasn't always easy making decisions, you know. Two Jews, three opinions. But the Sisterhood did so much of the work. We would put on affairs—dinner dances, luncheons, fashion shows. Once, we chartered a train car and took a whole gang to New York for a weekend. Such a ball. All kinds of things to bring in new people and raise money. The Sisterhood really was the glue that stuck it all together. That's how we all became such friends, we girls. We were so proud of that first temple building. It really made a statement, and your mother had such a hand in it."

"I guess I don't know anything about how the temple got built. I just remember it as always being there."

"I don't have to tell you Lily adored everything new and modern, and she had such good taste. That abstract stained glass was her idea. You didn't know? And then, years later when we expanded, those windows were just about the only thing we saved to use again in the new sanctuary. I still think of Lily whenever I see them. Of course, that was after she turned her back on us. But I don't go to services now, anyway. I can't drive anymore, that's why I'm moving, and what do I need with three bedrooms, plus a den and family room? If I had grandchildren...but of course, Lewis and Ken don't have kids. Gay people can be perfectly wonderful parents, I have no problem, and Ken is a darling man. But they're your age, so too late now. And they're only in Annapolis, an easy drive, so they have no reason to come stay with me. My new apartment has a bedroom and a den, that's plenty."

"What do you mean, turned her back on you?"

"Well, we hardly saw them over such a span of years, Sid and Lily, and people grow apart. That's natural. But it was already different that first time they came home from Taipei. Living over there had made her different, somehow. She was doing things that just seemed so strange to me—that I really couldn't accept. Whatever was she doing with that Portuguese man, for instance, going off to wherever that was while your father was someplace else. Your father! You could say he was always someplace else. God knows he was not the warmest man. Though I've seen plenty worse. And what? Life wasn't exciting enough for Lily already? Then, p.s., she wouldn't talk about it. She had written us most vividly about him at the time—visiting his family home. But then she acted like it had no significance. That whole episode was very strange, and it made us feel shut out. Me, anyway, I shouldn't speak for Rose—and poor Rose can't speak for herself now, either."

"I want to see her while I'm here. I was going to ask you. What's the situation? It's a nursing home she's in?"

"No darling, don't go to see her. She won't know you and if she says two words, they won't make any sense. It'll break your heart. She really went downhill fast, the last few years. Anyhow, I just felt shut out then by Lily. As if she thought that whatever had happened to her, I couldn't ever possibly understand. What, was I stupid? Or, since I'd never been in the Far East, there were things I wouldn't know. So I shouldn't bother to ask? And after all those wonderful letters, where she described everything and constantly said how she missed us and wished we were there with her.

"And maybe you wouldn't know this. But we had clubbed together, a few of us couples, to buy them a welcome home gift—tickets to High Holiday services. Because it so happened that she and Sid were back here right when the holidays fell, and we were so sure they would be thrilled to be together with all of us from the temple group again at that wonderful time of year. We had actually bought the tickets and presented them. They were staying downtown at the Sheraton Park, and we went to have dinner with them—Rose and Harry and me and Sol. We were so excited to see them for the first time in so long. We hugged and kissed and had dinner, and Harry presented them with the tickets. 'Thank you, thank you! How thoughtful and how darling.'

"And then comes the payoff. They simply don't attend. They don't say a word that they aren't coming. They actually just do not show up at the services, and we're looking around this way and that for them. What, they didn't feel like being

119

Jews anymore? That it's something you can cast off like last year's outfit? It was just the strangest thing. All her best friends. I have never figured it out to this day. Oh, we saw her two or three times after that, every couple of years when they came on home leave, I guess. Home leave? *Leave home*, they should call it. That's what Lily did. She was like a sister to us, and then she left and never came back. Lily had really changed."

She looked at me, expecting something.

I suppose that, had it ever occurred to me to ponder the dissipation of my mother's friendships, it should have struck me as curious. I opened my mouth to begin some sort of apology but knew before I let it out that I didn't understand any better than Esther did. And it wasn't up to me to apologize. Instead, I said, "Well, it was such a big change, finding ourselves in Taipei. So different—"

"Yeah, yeah, sure. I know." She interrupted me. "People like us just didn't travel to foreign countries then, though we've all been to Europe a million times now. And just about everybody I know has been to China, too. The real China, not Formosa. Anyway, to pick up and actually move to a place so backward and different in—what year was it? Open sewers, you had to boil your own drinking water—these things we had a hard time imagining. It seemed brave and a little crazy, even. But your parents were so excited to go—we were excited for them too. For you all."

The two of us sat silently for a moment. I picked up my coffee cup as if to drink and found that it was already empty. Esther said, "We had been so close. You wouldn't imagine— Lily and Rose and I—like three sisters. We were poor together, but we didn't know it. And if we had, we wouldn't have cared. You know, most of us weren't from Washington. Most of us came here during the Roosevelt years, because it was the Depression and there were New Deal jobs for smart kids. Sol had just graduated from Penn and was hired at Commerce. I didn't work, but Rose and your mother first met when they were both secretaries—at the War Department, isn't that right? Most of us had left our families and our hometowns for Washington, and then moving out to Bethesda or Silver Spring was something else again because we were city kids, just about all of us.

"But starting the temple was like finding a new family. And you children all grew up like cousins, you remember? It was 'Aunt Esther' and 'Aunt Rose' and 'Aunt Jeanette' and 'Aunt Lily' from all of you. The carpools to Hebrew School, all the families together for those Fourth of July picnics in Rock Creek Park, those seders we had together over here because our house was big enough for everybody. That really was unusual, wasn't it? That closeness our families had?

"Susie Kleinwald—wasn't she in your class? She lived on a hippie commune for years, you know—in Tennessee of all places—before she came to her senses and went back to college. She used to brag to Ann and Morty that she and her friends were inventing some revolutionary new way for people to be together. What new way, I don't even want to think. Where are those so-called friends now? Do they even send a greeting card? Susie hasn't seen any of them in years, I assure you. She had her own P.R. firm, you know. A big success. She just retired too. She's darling, a fabulous girl—lost her husband to liver cancer. You ought to call her while you're here.

"But our group, the temple founders, we stayed friends our whole lives. Well, except for when there was a divorce. You lose touch with one or the other. Of course, most of them are gone now, and most of the ones who aren't, you wouldn't wish their condition on your worst enemy. I'm fine. I just can't see well. It's assisted living where I'm moving, but I'll have my own kitchen and everything—a complete condo. They'll just be there if I need help, or if something happens.

"But I never understood why it changed with your mother."

* * *

Lily *had* changed. I can see that now, having read the letters. When we went to Taipei, she was fascinated, of course. Asia captured her from that morning when we had first crossed the International Date Line and stepped off a plane into the strangeness of Tokyo. But during those early months, she also longed for the familiar, for life as a young Bethesda matron. For her community, her stable social circle and its predictable rounds. For Esther and for Rose.

I really had no idea at the time that she was missing home so badly. We kids were nothing but dazzled by our new life, even by the things that horrified us—a live chicken having its throat slit in the street market, a barefoot man with two enormous loads suspended from a bamboo pole across his shoulders, our own occasional hideous blunder of stepping ankle-deep into the stinking muck of a benjo ditch. I clearly remember an aura of encouragement and support for that fascination and engagement coming from Lily. She was always eager for excursions to places of interest, for spontaneous detours, for engaging strangers, even when there was nobody present who could interpret. And then, as we came to feel at home in Taipei, she was happy for us to go off exploring on our own. I see now, from her letters, that she was afraid of the things she didn't know about or know how to respond to—the WASPiness of the diplomatic culture, the miasma of poverty outside our walls, the bellicose Reds just over the horizon. But she concealed all that very well behind her curiosity, her careful presentation and bright affect. And by the time those first two years abroad had passed, she had changed absolutely.

It can't be that she lacked the skills of friendship. In Taipei, she worked to make new ones—Coletta and Gladys—but Esther would have agreed that Lily also knew how to walk away from friendship. What made her do that? By the end of that first tour in Taipei, her eagerness for home leave was no longer about renewing her ties to Washington. It was about perpetuating a new life that was entertainingly cosmopolitan, and perhaps it was a little bit about showing that life off. That first time on home leave was her chance to circumnavigate the globe—her first of several. Few Bethesda housewives had accomplished that by 1959, or even today. She was basking in a milieu that furnished exotic luxury, mild intrigue, the glow of moral superiority from charitable endeavors, and the romance of international travel. And perhaps romance, itself. Airliners and ocean liners, visits to storied places. To Paris and Venice. To the Taj Mahal. To Macau.

And then there's: "Your father! You could say he was always someplace else."

The women were like sisters—Lily, Esther, Rose. I think each of them thought of the others' husbands as family, too, but more like cousins, people you might be close to, and get along with, but might not have chosen. There were always hugs upon meeting and parting, and a warm bath of shared experience and belonging whenever the families were together. But I don't think the men would have described each other as brothers. And I doubt that they were as intimate as the women. But, as a rule, men weren't very close back then. Maybe men aren't now, either. The species hasn't evolved that far, although the truth is that I don't quite know any men now, so I shouldn't assume.

Once she was in Taipei, it seems that Lily realized she no longer had her girlfriends to rely on, and that my father wouldn't fill in for them. Her self-reinvention for life in the Foreign Service, her abandonment of the old friends, and her substitution of new ones, Rocky included, are all part of one interconnected shift, which eventually rendered Sid unnecessary. Aside from his being the proximate cause for her presence in Asia, the standard from which her bright new pennant could snap in the breeze.

As for Sid, even when he was present, there was always distance. Sid loved jigsaws and crosswords and math puzzles, partly for the intellectual challenge, but mainly because they let him be in the room without communicating to anybody else. Maintaining the required concentration was always his excuse. When tables were formed for bridge, Sid was always the first to volunteer, eager for those long silent moments of calculation that the game provides. In Taipei, Edith Mencken was his usual partner of choice—quiet, composed Edith who was such a contrast to her husband, Brad. Brad of the perpetually flowing cocktail bar and glad-handing banter, Brad who actually seemed interested in people. I can't say that Edith wasn't, but if she was, it wasn't visibly clear. Edith was more of a watcher. But at the bridge table, she relaxed. For her, as for Sid, the game offered both structure and protection from the crowd.

The only puzzle my father never successfully solved was the puzzle of Rocky. Or perhaps he did. What makes me think I would know?

In memory, I see my father in Taipei as a Magritte painting. Just a bowtie, heavy black-framed reading glasses, a pencil, and the Sunday *New York Times*—all suspended in space around the head and shoulders of a missing person. Sid was addicted to the *Times'* crossword puzzle. He had an expensive airmail subscription, just so he could do the puzzle. The issues nevertheless arrived a week or more late, so it was rare that he actually worked the puzzle on Sundays, when we would typically have been out on the water or on some excursion to the countryside. Or he might have been away on TDY, off doing whatever he was off doing.

He died before the advent of the fax machine, a pity for him because he surely would have managed to get hold of a stapled eight-page daily digest the *New York Times* used to publish called *TimesFax*, which included the daily crossword. This form of daily news fix was eventually rendered obsolete by their website that's updated every few minutes and available everywhere. But before that, *TimesFax* went to Type A persons wherever they were in the world, so they could continue to feel themselves in daily control of the world. And high-end resorts would put a stack of them on the breakfast buffet each morning, so their guests could still feel in control—even while they were putatively away from it all, barefoot in Bali or wherever.

Sid: a bowtie, and reading glasses that he sometimes allowed to slide down his nose so he could glance over at us with the paper still held up in front of him like a shield. From my father, I inherited the skill of shielding myself. He responded to most things—encounters, information, obstacles—with reserve, an instinctive concealment. Reserve, in his case, qualified him for a profession of secrecy. With me, it's more like withholding; I may tell, sooner or later. I probably will. But the instinct is to hold back, all the same.

My father bestowed this skill from a distance, a stance I believe he generally maintained despite his functional partnership with my mother. I have since transmuted this skill into my own great expertise at solitude. Skill at maintaining distance is not a trait I would recommend passing on to your children, if you have a choice. You want them to have—the world needs them to have—empathy and heart. But people don't always manage to bequeath the legacy they intend, and we don't usually get to choose our inheritance.

* * *

During that second tour in Taipei, Sid continued to do TDYs in Saigon, and occasionally in Vientiane and Phnom Penh. Only later did I realize that I never quite knew what for. Or, for that matter, what his actual job was. He always had opaque titles like Field Director or Supervisor of Operations. Shades of the Foreign Operations Administration. I suppose he was a watcher of some sort too, officially but clandestinely. Maybe Edith Mencken was also one. I mean, actually working for the government as one, without anybody save possibly Brad, and maybe Sid and Rocky, knowing.

Surely there were some women spooks then—some of the wives? I know there were later on, since more than one crossed my path. At least one tried to recruit me, I just now remembered, when I was visiting my folks one time, in Jakarta.

126

An acquaintance of Lily's, she invited me for lunch and a drive through Menteng, a sedate garden suburb that had originally been inhabited by Dutch colonial functionaries, before Indonesia got its independence in 1949. Touring the leafy, rationally platted streets of a district of elegant villas within a city of such dense chaos was unremarkable midday entertainment for a visiting young woman like me with a Foreign Service background. It was also an activity that could provide cover. We stopped for coffee. "You must hear things at that camp on the Thai border," she mused idly, stirring her brew. "You must meet a lot of people who have stories, know things that could be of value to our side."

I said, "Yes, I hear a lot of stories. Of burning villages. Is that the sort of thing you think would be of value to our side?"

It was actually during those same years—our early years overseas, those Kennedy years—that I vaguely began to sense that politics and intrigue, more than beneficent global charity, were the matrix in which we USAID families were suspended. I did read *The Ugly American* during that first year in Taipei, as Lily mentions, and also *The Quiet American*—the much better novel of the two, subtler but more perceptive about the politics and scheming. Even though the late Fifties and early Sixties was a period of lull between the two Indochinese wars—the French one and ours—those books helped locate Vietnam for me at the heart of what I knew about America and Asia. They imprinted Vietnam in my consciousness as the template for our bungling relations with the world ever since. But as a teenager, I didn't know that Vietnam would stamp itself so indelibly on my family, too.

Lily became perfectly comfortable in Asia. That she could eventually do so was clear even in her early letters as she described missing her old friends at home with such a pang. It might seem paradoxical, but she became a Europhile too. After her first taste, she always insisted that they go on home leave through Europe, even though they'd have to fly economy to do so; State would cover the cost of first-class travel via the most direct route, across the Pacific, but they were free to apply that amount however they wanted to make their trip.

Lily was especially enchanted by the remnants of France she found while they lived in Saigon—the bakeries and the influence on the cooking, the street names, the colonial-era architecture. But she was fully ready to leave there by 1965. Not because of the increasingly close menace of bombings and battles, or monks and nuns burning themselves alive in protest, or farms and villages being napalmed from the air, but because of the acceleration that she sensed was coming to the city, the increasingly frenzied influx of Americans and Americanisms. With them, they'd bring inevitable changes that would rub out those romantic traces of France and *la mission civilisatrice.* When she and Sid transferred to Jakarta from Bangkok in '69, after two tours in Thailand, she appreciated the hints of the Dutch there too. Though they were fainter than the French residue in Saigon.

But Lily was also fascinated by the indigenous cultures she encountered in every post. She always took cooking and language classes, collected antiques and traditional crafts, had cocktail-dress versions of the national costume made to order. There also happened to be Chinese expat elites in Saigon, Bangkok, and Jakarta, longstanding Chinese communities with their temples built in traditional style, their restaurants and tailors, their lantern festivals and red paper dragons. All this layered on a certain familiarity, which resonated with her original take on Asia that had been acquired through a Chinese lens in Taipei.

Sid died quite unexpectedly at only 60 years old while they were living in Jakarta. Lily returned to Washington soon afterward, but she didn't stay long. She was deeply habituated by then to the tropics, to gin gimlets and boating parties. She toyed with resettling in the Caribbean so a semblance of that life could be approximated while allowing frequent visits home. St. John, Nassau, Montego Bay—she paid a few exploratory visits to those places. But each time, she changed her return ticket and flew back to D.C. early, bored to tears. She was deeply attached to Asia—its thrumming cities, its cultures that fascinated precisely because she could not fully understand them. She was particularly used to the cosmopolitan world that she had inhabited there. For a while, she considered whether that might be obtainable while living in England or France but concluded that it was too late for her to build an entirely new life apart from the social networks she'd been a part of in Taipei. Lily did not have a solitary nature—she feared loneliness, I should say. In the end, she sold the Bethesda house and moved to Hong Kong. People she knew from nearly 20 years in Asia were always passing through Hong Kong. She had been to Hong Kong plenty of times herself by then.

Lily liked Hong Kong because it was familiarly Chinese but was also reminiscent of New York in its scale and energy. It was intense, entrepreneurial, brash, precarious—given that it would revert from British to Chinese control by the end of the century—a place of smoke and mirrors and hurtling fun. They were still using rickety bamboo scaffolds to construct new buildings, even tall buildings, when she moved there in 1977, as had been the practice in every other Asian city she'd lived in or visited. She felt right at home there. She bought an apartment in Mid-Levels with a view down to Victoria Harbour. During her time there, she also became a regular visitor to a certain tile-floored villa in Macau.

* * *

It wasn't just Lily who was changed by that first tour in Taipei. All four of us were. "We were poor together," Esther said of our families, though it'd been a huge exaggeration. That was hardly true during the late Forties and early Fifties when she and Sol, Rose and Harry, Lily and Sid, and the rest of their gang were buying Buick convertibles and building suburban houses in Bethesda and Silver Spring. All of their parents had been immigrants from Eastern Europe, speakers first of Yiddish and possibly second of Polish or Russian. Some of their mothers, including Lily's, were virtually illiterate. They'd arrived through Ellis Island with only what they carried, even if in some cases that might have included a packet of rubles or a couple of diamonds sewn into the hem of an overcoat.

That generation of immigrants struggled for a foothold, which was rocked soon enough by the Depression. But their kids grew up as fluent Americans with free public-school educations and their own more-confident purchase. In the case of my parents and those who became their friends, this was achieved by migrating to Washington for government jobs— secure employment with middle-class pay. It was hardly poverty. Many of those friends eventually became rich. Sol Eisenstein left the Department of Commerce and, with Esther's brother, a born salesman, founded a rental-car outfit that became a national brand. Rose Neuberg's husband, Harry, an attorney at the Department of Labor, quit to pioneer the new specialty that was shopping center law, and ended up with a piece of the action in malls up and down the East Coast.

My father only ever had a civil servant's salary, and even a high-level one was nothing compared to what Sol or Harry eventually pulled down every year—not accounting for the free housing and travel and the endless other blandishments and perks that Lily describes in her letters. In posts like Saigon and Jakarta, there was even extra "hardship" pay, due to having to deal with the threat of missiles and grenades, student riots, malaria, and leprosy. There was hardship pay even in Taipei in '57. Maybe because there wasn't any television there, who knows? Our life in Taipei didn't seem beset by hardship, to me. Still, it was cash up front. When Sid died, beyond the nest egg they had built up over those years, he left Lily the reliably adequate pension of a Foreign Service widow. And when, finally, she sold the Bethesda house, which they'd rented for all the years, she got 20 times what they'd originally paid for it. Then she bought her mountainside perch in Hong Kong before property and living costs blasted off there on their own stratospheric trajectory. In 1977, when she settled there, Lily could still have a fabulous cocktail outfit tailored in Hong Kong for under $50.

It would have been accurate for Esther to say that, as young families, they all had considerably more modest means than they came to have later. But that's the thing about money amnesia, which I have only observed in others, since I have never had much wealth of my own. People never think they have enough, and since having money does not insulate them from anxiety but, because the memory of discomfort diminishes, when they look back at a time when they had much less, it can seem as if they had almost nothing. But the memory of financial stress, and of straining to keep up appearances, fades, allowing them to recall those prior years as incalculably happier times. In Bethesda during the Fifties, chuck steak was going for 49 cents a pound at the Giant supermarket. It was so cheap that our mothers often broiled steak for breakfast to fortify us for the school day. Although it was chuck, not tenderloin, this was hardly the breakfast of impoverished schoolchildren. When you reach the place of affluence where you are routinely able to eat tenderloin, what you should logically remember about chuck is the gristly bits that get caught in your teeth. But I recall those steak breakfasts as extravagant and languid, like the buffets we served ourselves from on the *Lurline* as the placid, gleaming white liner steamed into the tropics.

In the Foreign Service, we kids acquired a taste for, along with the expectation of, luxury. In the context of our astonishing new reality, the ceaseless flow of access and treats was pleasurable and interesting. But it also seemed unremarkable, precisely because it came to us with no effort. It was all just part of the experience. Flying adventures for a teenager arranged by a family acquaintance who ran the local airline. Seaside holidays at restricted-access beaches as guests of the host government. A mission car on call when we wanted to go swim at the Grand, indeed our very membership at the Grand. We couldn't have imagined these things from Bethesda, before we arrived in Taiwan, just as we couldn't have pictured the poverty of postwar Taipei. Jordy and I were not unaffected by the poverty. On the contrary, it became a decisive factor— fatally so, you might even say—in the paths we each chose to follow. But after our initial shock, the everyday conditions most people contended with in Taipei—pre-Asian-Tiger Taipei—quickly came to seem natural. Mere facts of life. Just how they lived, we might have said, as if living in poverty was a cherished local tradition.

As for our new existence as global aristocrats in training? That seemed normal, too. It was just how *we* lived. These days, that kind of blasé attitude is called entitlement, a word that usually drips with contempt. That attitude deserves contempt, especially when it emanates from people who did nothing to attain their lofty standards of living. I find them as obnoxious as anyone else does. But I'm here to say that an entitled lifestyle can consume you with insidious ease. And it isn't always necessarily conjoined with smugness. Sometimes, the entitled are simply oblivious; spoiled brats don't learn that they are spoiled if no one ever slaps them. Luxuries are narcotic—lulling and addictive—and when you're surrounded by them, consuming them as they endlessly present themselves to you, it requires an effort of consciousness and will to remember that there are other ways people are living, and that it may not be by their choice. And even having this insight about the realities of poverty is nothing compared to the effort that is required to try altering them.

I know about that ease of unconscious entitlement because I lived it. I know about the effort of breaking through it, too. I have spent half my adult life working in, and then managing, relief projects in Asia. That has meant dealing with the human wreckage of the Vietnam War, which ended in '75 but, like a Superfund site, continues to seep toxins—metaphorically and for real. Occasionally, my attention to the taint of that particular war has been diverted by some other war, or by an earthquake or tsunami emergency—those last two being oddly satisfying, perspective-restoring reminders that the processes of nature can be as calamitous to the masses as the misdeeds and stupidity of their leaders.

The other half of my career has been in the travel industry. Specifically, and I know this sounds crazy, in the luxury sector of international travel. I would burn out on one kind of work after a couple of years and then switch back to the other. Like relief work, hospitality could also be mighty challenging. It did, however, always come with air conditioning and clean linens and regular days off; you could drink the water. And not just the water that was bottled, chilled, sparkling, and imported from France, but the water that ran from the tap. In my resort jobs, unlike my relief jobs, there was always a tap, along with those chilled bottles of sparkling mineral water too. After the enervation of refugee camps and makeshift offices in provincial capitals and the seasonal rotations of mud and dust, working at a luxury spa resort felt almost therapeutic, as if I were a paying guest, myself.

The people skills required by these two occupations are oddly interchangeable. Both desperate, exhausted refugees and demanding, asshole tourists respond to a soothing tone and an attitude of service. I did hospitality work mostly in Asia. I tried the Caribbean, too, but didn't find that environment any more engaging than Lily did, possibly for the same reasons. My last job was as the concierge—okay, guest relations manager, I was never a formally certified concierge—at a boutique eco-resort in Australia. I enjoyed the irony of that property's costly simplicity: our guests, like so many homeless asylum seekers I had known, also slept in tents. My early years as a Foreign Service brat, an unthinkingly privileged consumer of luxuries and international travel, were a good preparation for this half of my professional life.

My knowledge of Chinese language and culture helped get me hired at the eco-resort—as it had also often come in handy in the relief work—since more tourists come to Australia now from China than from anyplace else. They come from Taiwan, which has become a wealthy country, with cities of glossy towers rising from streets where there were once benjo ditches. But they come in far greater numbers from what I still reflexively think of as "the Mainland," as if I'm still gazing toward it from Generalissimo Chiang's little island bastion; they come from what Esther called "the real China," where poverty still abounds, where getting rich is deemed to be glorious, and where the tiny fraction who succeeded in following that dictum is apparently large enough to keep the luxury resorts of Australia fully booked and profitable.

It was comforting and ironically restorative for me, having experienced such rough living and witnessed so much deprivation in my professional life, to be working in that artificially rusticated environment, with its whiff of moral superiority. I spent the formative period of my childhood in a milieu where offhand luxury was the norm, which is why I made a good guest relations person. I could understand what the entitled felt entitled to. But the implicit moral superiority of the "eco" aspect of the place was the source of irony. The place was obsessive about the sorting of paper and glass, the rinsing of bottles and cans for recycling. All the shellfish served was harvested right from our bay. Produce was grown in on-site gardens kept rich with composted food waste. And there we were in Australia with its reasonably admirable culture of environmental responsibility. But all the enlightened actions we could possibly have taken—*we* being a lavish ratio of 22 staff to 24 guests—would not have offset the carbon cost of one couple's roundtrip flight there from Beijing, even if they flew economy, which I assure you they did not. In the meantime, the thousands of refugees I tried helping through the mud and out of leaking tents to some kind of viable life—well, let's say the luckiest of them—are now only trying to get to a place from which they might afford a trans-Pacific flight to pay a visit to their homeland once before they die.

* * *

At the end of that first home leave, Lily and Sid had no hesitation about sending Jordy and me back to Hong Kong on our own. Really, there was no danger in our making the trip without our parents, no more than there had ever been in our stepping outside the gate in Taipei, where we would often hail a pedicab by ourselves or pick our way through the rainy season mud to the street market. We enjoyed the trip too. The long flights gave us time to settle into our pair of seats, at times pulling a blanket together over our heads like the clubhouse a pair of much younger siblings might contrive. This long trip engendered a rare moment of intimacy between us two, which was just about the last moment like that we ever shared. The stewardesses gave us special attention all the way—decks of cards, extra snacks.

And there were all the different kinds of planes we took, which I remember because of Jordy's obsession with them. We flew from Washington to Chicago on a Super-G Constellation. Its swooping lines and triple tail surely made it the most graceful-looking commercial aircraft ever built, though it was a deafening, shuddering beast in the air. From Chicago to Los Angeles, it was a Lockheed Electra turboprop, then we travelled by jet from there to Tokyo on a DC-8. "It's the airliner of tomorrow," Jordy said pompously and without irony, repeating something he'd read in a magazine ad. All those planes were new models to us, new birds for our life lists. From Tokyo to Hong Kong, we were on Cathay Pacific's Golden Dragon, which was really just an all-first-class DC-7 with fanciful livery and elaborate, multi-course Chinese meals—a historical oddity. That was the precise moment in time, 1959, when the turboprops and jets were coming into service, when air travel was beginning to be an everyday thing. I guess it still made sense at the time for an airline to dress up a single craft like that and market it as something rare. And passengers, long acclimated to infrequent departures, boring layovers and unexpected delays— and to not infrequent deadly crashes—would happily plan their itineraries around the two or three times a week this single brightly plumed creature flew their desired route.

The Golden Dragon stopped in Taipei, but we didn't get off. It landed before dawn and we slept through the refueling. But when the plane took off again and banked to the west, the day had grown light enough for us to awaken and look down at the city. We picked out the Grand Hotel on its mountainside, and the building downtown where the ICA offices were located. We had once stood on that roof to watch the Double Ten Day parade. We failed to pinpoint our own house resting on its narrow lane, which made me quite sad. I missed Taipei. I missed our freedom there, and the parade of delights and amazements—the sailing, the trips to sulfur spas and to temples where nuns with shaved heads served us tea. I missed being treated as a grownup by grownups like Rocky and Coletta, who probably didn't know how not to treat us like grownups, since they had no children of their own. I missed Hsiu.

The truth is that I resented being sent away to school in Hong Kong. I had loved Taipei. St. Botolph's was a good school academically that had a diverse international student body, which was an education in itself. We were fortunate to be there. But it was stuffy and strict. It wasn't much fun. I think Jordy felt the same sense of loss—of having been robbed, though the things he missed were more to do with the freedom to be a juvenile-delinquent-in-training and get away with it. He missed Hsiu too, no doubt. On that last leg of the long trip, from Taipei back to Hong Kong, our closeness dissipated. I grew depressed, and Jordy grew cranky. Returning to St. Botolph's for another year renewed our sense of resentment—of having been rejected, sent away.

For all of us Norells, the moment when we kids went away to school in Hong Kong marked the end of our life as a normal family, if we had ever been one. If there is such a thing in this world.

But Lily.

Whatever *was* she doing with that Portuguese man? Little as Esther understood about how and why Lily had changed, she seemed to think Rocky Perreira had a lot to do with it. It certainly must have looked that way from her distant vantage point, through the window of Lily's letters. It often looks that way to me, too, between the letters and my memories of Rocky, which still exude a seductive luster all these years later. Of course, if he's still alive, he can't possibly be the debonair, carefree Carey Grant simulacrum that he was. Grinning triumph from the deck of his sailboat, sartorially daring for the era in Bermuda shorts. He would be more than a century old now, shrunken, hardly gorgeous.

When scanned intensively, Lily's letters function like a prism. A prism splits and disperses light—useful for science, but not so much for personal history. Behind the letters' jaunty travelogue and linear narrative, I glimpse a shifting assemblage of fragments. I can see how this might have confounded Esther; Lily's letters did not depict the stable image that Esther could always count on seeing through the picture window of her Bethesda living room.

The letters suggest that Lily and my father were a good team. He was the newly minted Foreign Service officer meeting the multiple challenges of his first post with enthusiasm and competence. And that propelled him on to a successful career. The State Department doesn't give out medals the way the military does, but if it did, his chest would have been highly decorated by the time he died in Indonesia. Lily was, at first, the natural corollary—the resolute, soon enough to be consummate, Foreign Service wife who joined the International Women's Club, volunteered in various efforts and then discovered a devotion to the orphans of Asia. While at the same time, she could be mingling unflappably with admirals and ambassadors, personages from many countries, and American colleagues whom she may not have particularly cared for or chosen voluntarily to socialize with. She also maintained a household, though this was the easiest of the tasks, with Hsiu and Wei to do the work. All of that was carried out so my father could come and go just as his work demanded.

Hers was a profession in its own right, as generations of unpaid but accomplished diplomatic wives will tell you, and it was a requirement of their husbands' jobs, though unstated. Lily astutely noted early on that Gladys Walter, our next-door neighbor, did not *go in for charitable projects as such, but she just tries to make everyone happy.* Gladys played her supporting role by being a charming and energetic hostess, at whose house the bar was always open, thereby providing a needed venue and useful lubrication for social cohesion within the ICA ranks. Gladys was a drunk, as you may have deduced from mention of her champagne breakfast parties, although a high-functioning one who helped advance her husband's career. If she had been the type who drinks alone every afternoon with the shades drawn and doesn't make friends, the Walters' days in the Foreign Service would have ended long before we met them. Since then, there have been plenty of female Foreign Service officers—not just wives—and even Black ones like Coletta. Including Coletta. Yes, Coletta did not stay a secretary once advancement became a possibility for a Black person. And now we have had women as Secretary of State, too, and even a Black woman Secretary of State. I suppose this aspect of that life may have changed, the unpaid professional wife part. I'm only telling it like it was.

While in her unofficial role as patron of orphans, Lily was not above bending rules to accomplish what she wanted. Flirting with the logistics guy to redirect crates of canned food or medical supplies, or pulling Sid's rank with the motor pool guy for the use of a van to take children on an outing to the zoo. Sid would chide her mildly when he found out about these sleights of hand. Of the two of them, he was the one with a sworn obligation to be seen playing by the rules. So much for that, given that he was a spook—although I suppose that particular field of specialization has its own set of rules, which he probably did follow.

Lily and Sid did not do confrontation. They certainly talked enough: considering options, making plans. I remember collegial discussions between them, which I overheard at intervals of years on visits to wherever they were living, about potential next posts, shipping arrangements for a new car, home leave plans. They were mutually confident partners in the Norell family enterprise. I do not ever recall any visible expression of tension between them—which perhaps reflected my father's remote temperament instead of her expressive one. It begs the question of why she acceded to that particular family-corporate culture. I also do not recall ever seeing much physical expression of connection between them. Or endearments. I can't help picturing Lily and Sid asleep in twin beds. Though as far as I know, that wasn't ever the way their room was actually furnished.

Just a trick of memory.

And that Portuguese man, as Esther called him with distaste. For all Esther's liberal sophistication, which really would have been hard not to acquire from residing in Bethesda for the six decades after 1950—"been to Europe a million times," "gay people can be perfectly wonderful parents"—she remained an essentially small-minded girl from Newark who never went beyond high school or held a paying job. She was uneasy about anybody who originated from outside the urban, Northeastern, working-class, Jewish-immigrant world—its leftishness notwithstanding—in which she and my parents and their cohort grew up. She'd had a hard time over Lily's friendship with Coletta, too.

Rocky Perreira remained in Lily's life—in all of our lives—after Taipei. He stayed in Asia, and we all ran into him repeatedly. In Lily's case, the encounters were intentional, and were never meant to be hidden. I can't keep precise track of his postings or movements after we first knew him in Taipei. Years later, Coletta described Rocky to me as being "permanently on the loose. Professionally so, you might say." There was a wink and a nod in her tone when she said it, an inflection I had long ago come to decode. Rocky's path did not precisely overlay Lily and Sid's, but he also served in Bangkok and Saigon. If Lily were in Hong Kong to shop, or to see us, or was en route to or from home leave, he might meet her for a day of sailing among the islands on his cousin's boat or for a visit to Macau. Despite whatever his official duties may have been, Rocky was always able to travel at whim.

He was her great friend. She always presented him as such, and if she had any idea that other people might have raised an eyebrow, she never dignified it with a visible reaction. For me, running into Rocky always seemed to be a coincidence, but that's how it seemed to her too on that first trip to Hong Kong after Coletta had returned to Taipei and left her there alone. *What should happen but our friend Rocky Perreira showed up at my hotel.*

I can't place exactly when his official role changed, but at a certain point Rocky shifted from working for the State Department as a cultural attaché to working for Air America as—I think it was—Director of Marketing. You might think that the new job would have amounted to pretty much the same thing. However, Air America was a subsidiary of Civil Air Transport, whose vice president had been Rocky's boating pal Brad Mencken. And CAT was actually owned by the Central Intelligence Agency. The CIA was also Air America's principal customer. Air America staff actually used to refer to the CIA in general, and to the local CIA operations officer, as "the customer." The other, lesser, customer was USAID. So, marketing can't have required much of Air America's effort; the "airline" did not need to attract other "customers." And in the late Sixties, with the war out of control in Saigon, I don't imagine State was putting a lot of effort into genteel educational and cultural programming of the sort Rocky had done in Taipei, although that had only been a cover for whatever his real job had been.

I ran into Rocky by chance in '68 or '69—or perhaps it's just that he wanted it to appear by chance—in the lobby of the Hotel Le Royal in Phnom Penh, when I was there for a few days' break from my first exhausting stint at refugee work. I had not seen him for a long time. We were having a drink and he suddenly said, "Are you free tomorrow? Let me show you something you'll never forget." And we flew—in an Air America helicopter, just the two of us and a pilot, just for the afternoon—to Angkor Wat. There was no tourist presence to speak of at Angkor Wat back then, apart from a few intrepid backpackers and researching scholars. Most of the ancient ruins of the city were still smothered in a mat of jungle. I know it is easy to visit there now. Plenty of it has been made accessible to tourists, and quite a developed infrastructure has risen up with all kinds of hotels, including the deluxe sort that I have worked for. I was offered jobs there more than once. But I've never gone there again. I saw it *back when*, you see. I saw it before. I saw it with Rocky in a way that would be impossible to replicate, or top, and not just because of the chopper ride. Also because it was Rocky doing the showing.

I can be suspicious of what Rocky made a career doing, but I can't entirely mistrust him. I know he didn't always tell the truth. Not telling the truth was his profession, or let's say his ability to tell untruths with finesse was what qualified him for his job. While off the job, Rocky was still a charmer. Charmers are often suspect, for good enough reasons. But I can't mistrust his warmth, or his enthusiasm, or the genuine pleasure he took in people. In us. In me. In Lily. And how can I say she didn't deserve that?

* * *

The craftsman bungalow in the Berkeley hills that Coletta retired to was modest, an echo of her tiny Japanese house in Taipei. But it had a glorious view over the Oakland flats, where she had been a child, as well as the Bay Bridge and San Francisco. I visited her there on my way back to Asia from that trip to Washington after Lily died in 1988. It was one of those glassy, clear days that belong to a California winter, when we could see across the bay to the city and—in our minds' eyes, anyway—all the way to the Pacific.

Coletta said, "Your mother was an odd bird. A rare bird. People saw her as supremely confident. To be sure, she was unflappable—at least that's how she always appeared. And in the Foreign Service that really counts. She quickly understood the role and took it up."

"It's nothing like what she came from," I said.

"That may be. But still she was an innocent. A naïf, one could almost say. A curious naïf. That's was her appeal to people like me, to people like Rocky. Oh yes, Rocky and I are alike in certain ways. Outsiders within that small world, both of us."

"That's nonsense, Coletta."

"Okay, we were officially inside. We had standing because of our jobs, but we were also different from everyone else. Back in Taipei, I'm talking about. You can see what I mean, if you think back. Both of us were unmarried, to begin with. Unusual enough, there and then. And both, well, extraordinary. Our backgrounds. I, being African-American. Mind you, most African countries were still colonies in the Fifties, so it was the Brits, the French, and the Portuguese who spoke for them. There were no Black ambassadors from places like Nigeria. Not yet. And aside from some enlisted men at the Air Force base, I was possibly the only Black person in the city."

"I guess you're right about that."

"And Rocky, with his rather blurred origin story. His—how should I put it—malleable autobiography. Rocky always wore that big grin on his face. I couldn't afford to appear as anything other than pleased and smiling, either. 'Pleased to meet you,' 'Pleased to be your administrative assistant,' 'Pleased you invited me to the party.' Certainly, I couldn't be seen to be less than *pleased* in those years in Taipei, where I was so junior, and, I might also add, so female and so Negro. But truly, I *was* pleased. Pleased, though rather isolated. We both were isolated. I, by my race and my necessary pleasantness. Rocky by being suaver than anyone on Earth could possibly be, and thus so difficult to pin down."

"I've never thought about it that way. What I remember is how much a part of things you both were. Integrated—sorry, I wasn't trying to joke."

"You would remember it that way because we were both becoming close to your mother, so we saw your family often. It was different for each of us, Rocky and I. I was frequently not invited by people—I don't mean Lily—or invited out of

145

obligation. And my exception from the norm was only enhanced when I took up with Scotty. The fellow who ran the language school? You remember?"

"Whatever happened to Scotty?"

"He got into politics, eventually ending up in the legislature. Died pretty young though. Lung cancer, I think. But we were already no longer in touch, long before that. Anyway, I suppose if he had been a Mainlander or from an influential family, then dating him might have made me more valuable socially. But since he was Taiwanese and at the time a political nobody, associating with Scotty didn't do anything good for my status. And Rocky. Rocky paradoxically was insulated by his very bonhomie. His *clubability*, one could call it. Or maybe what I should say is that he used that aura to insulate himself. One of those great guys everybody loves to be with, but nobody ever really gets to know. It's a type, isn't it?"

"Except for Lily. Lily got to know him."

"Yes, she did. Now your mother was always very correct, socially—and was often at pains to be. But she did not care about people's social cachet. You disagree? Well, I suppose she was impressed by status, generally speaking. And by style, certainly. We did love to shop together, the two of us, and she had such good taste. And as I said, she grasped protocol. And when she was faced with someone truly outside of her own experience, such as an earnest Black girl, for example? The first Black person she ever met on vaguely equal terms. Or a Macanese-American, another rara avis, too attractive to be unattached yet permanently on the loose? Lily looked right through the received wisdom about people like Rocky and me. She looked right at us. Believe me, you felt as if everybody else in the room had dematerialized and you were alone with her. It was the power of her interest. Her acknowledgment—the inquiry she projected. You were something she had never encountered, but that she had to understand. It was quite touching. Moving. Hard to resist. A kind of magnetism. Mutually so. I've never put it this way before, but it was as if my unfamiliarity, Rocky's singularity, exerted a certain pull on Lily. Her submission to it wielded a force of attraction back upon each of us."

The afternoon sun was beginning to fill the room with glare. Coletta got up with some difficulty—at 76, she was facing a hip replacement—to lower the blinds and switch on a lamp. "I think Lily had a lamp like that," I said.

"She certainly did. We bought the pair together in Bangkok, I think that was. We did that sometimes. I still have a jade bracelet that's a match to one of hers. Do you have that bracelet? No? I wonder where it went. We had so much fun, Lily and me. She was a real friend. You know that. No matter where in Asia I was posted or where your parents were, and even after she settled in Hong Kong, Lily's was where I always tried to be for Thanksgiving or for my birthday. I'm very sentimental about my birthday, don't you remember?"

"Ha! Those ice cream cakes. Didn't Hsiu make everybody an ice cream cake on their birthday?"

"Yes. It's an Australian thing, you know. Ice cream cake rather than ice cream *and* cake, like us. He learned it when he had his first job working for the Aussies. There was something so permanent about being in Lily's space, despite the fact that the houses, the apartments—the countries—changed every few years. She always had a list drawn up when I arrived, of shops to scour and tailors to visit. And there was Hsiu as a permanent fixture in every one of those kitchens, more reliable a presence than even your father."

"You know Lily left Hsiu her apartment?"

"No. That's touching to hear. He's such a treasure. So devoted so early to your mother that he was willing to forever overlook her loss of face for bringing Scotty, a lowly Taiwanese, into the household. And having to wait on Scotty at table. He hadn't cared about me being Black. There was no instruction in Chinese upbringing to denigrate Black people. In fact, Hsiu was always especially sweet to me, almost protective. I think he rather pitied me. He was afraid I would never marry."

I looked at my watch and explained that I would have to be going. She made me wait at the door, disappeared, and then returned with the bracelet. "You should have this, Lauren. You should wear more jewelry anyway, honey. It becomes you." She slipped it onto my wrist. "She was a real friend to Rocky, too, your mother. She may have been his only real friend. What? Lovers? Oh, do you think so?"

* * *

Yes, Hsiu went with my parents from Taipei to Saigon, and then everywhere else. He even moved to Hong Kong to keep house for Lily after Sid died, after she spent that futile year trying to live back "home" on the other side of the globe before giving up and becoming a permanent expat in Asia. I think it was quite unusual for Foreign Service people to take servants from one post to another. There certainly was never a labor shortage wherever you were sent in Asia. And I suppose his cooking and household management must have been a little tentative at the start in each new location, until he got to know the markets and tradesmen and the fixers. But for him, as for Lily, the presence of substantial Chinese communities in all those subsequent posts must have provided fast grounding. He was always able to quickly find a Chinese amah to work with him in the house. He hired locals only for the truly menial and grimy work—tending the garden, feeding the boiler, washing the car.

Hsiu was an odd duck, too. Hsiu Bo Lin. Gentle Rain Hsiu, he told us it meant, without exactly inviting the intimacy of our calling him by his given name. He was really too smart and too well-bred to be a cook, even if it was for a, ahem, "highest class" American family like ours, as he always described us. And he surely had the education and the class background—if not the actual social connections—to have established himself in business or government. But I think he had been too deeply traumatized by his escape from the Mainland.

He was the only member of his immediate family who got out as the Communists were taking over. And then he heard news—or rumors, trickling out in fragments as they did in those years when China was almost as sealed off as North Korea has remained—about how badly his people had been treated. Supposedly, his father had been beaten in public for having been a successful merchant. And it'd been Hsiu's sister who was forced to do the beating, perhaps aided by some helpful comrades from the neighborhood committee. The old man was beaten unconscious and died shortly after. The mother and sister were then stripped of everything they had and were sent into the netherworld of collective farms. Hsiu never learned anything more of them, as far as I know.

Sometime in 1958, Time magazine put an image of Mao Tse-tung on their cover. At that time, Jordy and I both had a comic book grasp of the situation on the Mainland; Taiwan, we learned by rote at the International School, was the real China. Red China was just an illusion. Jordy got the smart-assed idea to show the magazine to Hsiu and took it into the kitchen. "Do you know who this is?" he asked, expecting Hsiu to find it amusing. That was the only time I ever saw Hsiu get angry. It happened instantaneously, frighteningly. His invective was in wild Chinese well beyond my beginner's comprehension. This was before we went to St. Botolph's, where Jordy's formal introduction to Chinese history ignited the conscious anti-Communist passion that burned in him forever after.

This incident with Hsiu has a lot to do with why I myself could not become a leftist when I was a student at Michigan in the Sixties. Michigan had been the birthplace of SDS, Students for a Democratic Society—the organization that became a voice for America's young radicals of the day. Central to its early ideals were "participatory democracy" and the building of "an interracial movement of the poor." These, I could embrace; there wasn't that big a conceptual leap for me later on from the idea that it would be good to organize against poverty and for civil rights, to the idea that it would be good to help destitute refugees. But when people around me at the University of Michigan started glorifying Castro and waving Mao's little book of brainless quotations and calling themselves Communists, I always thought of Hsiu and looked around for the nearest exit.

Aside from that one outburst, the rest of the time, and I mean for the *entire* time, whenever I saw him over the many decades, Hsiu seemed utterly placid. He was always simultaneously warm and reserved. If Lily was as unflappable as Coletta described her, perhaps her ability to maintain that equilibrium was bolstered by his consistent presence and fixed emotional temperature. There was something not right about it in him. It just wasn't normal. Although, it was perfect majordomo behavior, ideal for the running of a smooth household. This mildly self-effacing but highly responsible role of chief servant of an American diplomatic household gave him a place to hide.

He was an excellent domestic manager, but he wasn't so fabulous in the kitchen, despite how Lily raved in her letters. She wrote, *He is an outstanding cook, and boy are my kids having a ball. He bakes daily—pies, cookies, rolls, biscuits. I am exerting great willpower, as you can imagine.* Of course, we were all impressed with being catered for and waited on. And those early Chinese dinners he made us were extra fun—learning to use chopsticks, the rice bowl, the little dishes of sauce—his were among our first authentic experiences of the cuisine. But he had a very limited repertoire. The centerpiece dish of all his Chinese dinners consisted of slivers of beef and green pepper in a brown sauce, which was decent enough. But its very recurrence as an exemplar of that endlessly varied cuisine belied his limitations. Of course, none of us knew much about Chinese food so early on, and I can only judge Hsiu's cooking as mediocre now because I've spent so much of my life in Asia. I've tasted the miracles that the regional ingredients can produce when prepared with a cleaver and wok. If there isn't a war or flood or famine on, to interfere with dinner plans.

Hsiu was quite a handsome man, and young when we first knew him. He was graceful and trim—I used to see him in the early mornings from the window of my bathroom, which looked out onto the service yard at the back of the kitchen, doing calisthenics. We never knew him to be involved with a woman, but there was a succession of younger men. As he grew older, the young men seemed more and more like boys in comparison. Sometimes, this would be a part-time member of the household staff, a houseboy or gardener. Other times, the companion was just known to us as Hsiu's Friend. There was a world in the servant's wing that we were not a part of and didn't inquire into. *Re your mother's kind inquiry as to the type of stove we have, tell her, how should I know?* Our vagueness regarding life on the other side of the kitchen door extended to its social relations, and that deliberate unfamiliarity of course is generally useful in the situation of servants and employers. I understand that homosexuality was a relatively open and accepted thing in China's long history. Until it was met with horror by European imperialists and Christian missionaries in the 18th and 19th Centuries, and when their revulsion was taken up by Westernized "modernizers" like Sun Yat-sen and Madame Chiang in the 20th. I think this is another reason why Hsiu gladly went along with Lily and Sid after Taipei. It was probably easier for him to be who he was, given the opportunity to re-create himself in a new place every few years. The lack of permanent ties and the dominion he always had over the staff quarters of the house gave him space, both literal and figurative.

Hsiu was avuncular and protective toward us kids when we first knew him. Lily described that incident when Hsiu and I marched down the lane to liberate our little dog as if I were the commander and he was merely carrying out my orders, but that's not how it happened. I was distraught when he came back from the market and announced that he'd discovered the dognapper to be one of our neighborhood squatters. It was he who organized our expedition for my benefit and out of concern for how Jordy would react when he found out; I don't think Hsiu cared a fig for the puppy. It had felt wonderfully supportive as a young girl to walk into such a bizarre situation accompanied by this confident young man, whose attitude was patrician, cloaked in his crisp white cook's jacket and his disdain for the people in those shacks.

Though I think he loved Jordy even more than me. Perhaps he was in love with Jordy. As I say, Hsiu had a thing for younger men. Jordy would have been 13 and 14 that first year in Taipei, when he was in the throes of raging hormones, and then a good-looking 15-, 16-, and 17-year-old when he saw Hsiu while on school holidays over the following years. And Jordy was a bit of a flirt, as a kid. That gradual half-smile of his might have been read as an invitation.

Perhaps they were even lovers, those two. I wouldn't say Jordy was gay, but what I know of his sexual history was that it was certainly tumultuous enough to have encompassed a teenage tryst with the cook. It's none of my business, really, and doesn't bear much thinking about—who likes to envision their family members having sex?—but still, I wonder. Hsiu's serene affect shattered when he heard about Jordy's suicide. I was wrong—it was twice that I witnessed a rupture in Hsiu's placidity. Perhaps Hsiu nurtured a hopeless love for Jordy, which was one more reason for him to follow Lily and Sid all over Asia. And then both Jordy and Sid had died in the same year. Perhaps this double tragedy cemented his ties to Lily. So it made perfect sense to both of them that he should later rejoin her in Hong Kong to serve as retainer and cook for the rest of her life, and that she should later leave him the apartment in Mid-Levels. He remained there after her death and is living in it to this day, Hsiu Bo Lin, Gentle Rain, the haughty, delicately handsome, serenely aging Chinese bourgeois he was originally destined to be—gazing placidly over the hectic city from Lily's balcony on the mountainside.

* * *

Jordy died in 1975. So he never had the chance to read Lily's letters, to have these brittle, discolored pages provoke some reflection on how Taipei changed things for us. But Jordy wasn't a reflective person. Jordy put a great deal of energy into forgetting, as a matter of fact—and the older he got, the more desperately he did so, though he only lived to be 31. I am now over twice that age. And I remember plenty. Although I should be honest and acknowledge that my impressions of what happened, and why—of dialogues, motivations, emotional nuances—may be only fragments of truth by now, glued together with imagination. I do vividly recall images that are surely real—scenes, settings, snapshot glimpses. The gondolas on Green Lake. The Little Sea Hut on the far shore, where we clambered up to have tea in glasses with jasmine flowers aswhirl. My father's head swathed in gauze, blanked out, an apparition. The hammered metal of the ocean's surface from 17,000 feet out the porthole of a DC-6 when I was 15, and the ocean's smooth sheen from 36,000 in a 747 on so many later trans-Pacific crossings. Of course, I've misplaced a great many details. I couldn't tell you how many times I've flown across that ocean. Jordy never lost track. He might have, had he lived long enough, grown up enough to let go the need to keep count. But maybe not. As Lily frequently pointed out, Jordy was crazy for airplanes. Jordy was hellbent on flight.

Rocky Perreira tried to keep an eye on Jordy during those visits he occasionally paid to St. Botolph's, where Jordy's bruises were not, in fact, acquired on the rugby field. Rocky, despite trying, was a bit too romantic a figure, just a little too much all smiles all the time for all-comers, to wax convincingly avuncular. He conveyed the requisite worldliness but lacked the necessary bracing sternness. I suppose he tried anyway out of his devotion to Lily. Despite the ultimate waste of his efforts, I can say with gratitude that I don't think Rocky ever gave up on Jordy.

As for Lily, when it came to Jordy, the facile explanation always sufficed. Jordy's conflicts with our father? Normal male teen behavior, what's a mother to do? Incidents of hooliganism at the International School in Taipei? To her, it was always the military kids with duck's-ass haircuts. Even though Jordy was the one who lit those firecrackers under the pedicab that one time after school. I was there to see it, while waiting for the mission car that would take us home. Such incidents seemed to escape Lily's notice. Firecrackers shoved up the assholes of stray dogs, their fuses then lit. The dealing of marijuana escaped her notice entirely, since it wasn't even the Sixties yet and he was only 14. Middle-class American parents didn't yet know that pot was something to worry about, and maybe, back home in the States, it would have been too early for the drug to have entered Jordy's life. Anyway, I don't know if pot can really be blamed as a gateway drug to harder stuff—it was never for me— but I do know that my brother did drugs young and that he did eventually stumble down that spiral until he was undone. He did drugs. But mostly, as an adult, he drank.

Many people sought to help Jordy over the years. Despite his mediocre school record, he was accepted at the University of Maryland after St. Botolph's—probably because our legal address was still Bethesda, and entrance standards were low for in-state residents. When he tried to transfer to the Air Force Academy after his first semester in College Park, Brad Mencken, the CAT vice president with the famous cabin-cruiser cocktail bar, who was a decorated former Air Force flyer, tried pulling strings. But Jordy lacked the grades, never mind credible character references. And when he flunked out of Maryland the following year and showed up back in Taipei, it was Brad again, at Rocky's urging no doubt, who arranged a job for him at CAT's head office.

Lily and Sid were in Saigon then, from where they could continue to remain oblivious, and I was a senior at Michigan, so I didn't see it with my own eyes. But I still corresponded, as I do to this day, with my Taipei girlfriend Rosemary Ling. Correspondence in ink on paper was so common then as to be totally unremarkable—you didn't have to be stationed halfway around the globe to have that habit. Letters, pages and pages, thoughtfully composed. And you waited for replies, for hopefully-thick envelopes, waited sometimes for weeks in pleasurable or even tortured anticipation in case there was some juicy or urgent development you craved word of. Picture Lily, in Taipei, impatient for Sid to come home for lunch on mail days. In those early days when she still wanted to hear from Rose and Esther, I mean. Writing letters was just something you did, an important part of living—but I don't have to explain this. Lily's letters demonstrate it perfectly well. You saved up anecdotes and apercus and planned your reply like...like—well,

156

like nothing anybody does now. Sorry. Excuse me. I'm old. Go ahead, click send, click delete. Reposition your earbuds.

Anyway, Rosemary and I still write, though only two or three times a year now. It's been a long time since we've seen each other, and our letters have become rather pro forma. Lily also wrote to me throughout her life, until the brief period near the end when she was too unwell to focus. Her letters were always as chatty and vivid—and as self-absorbed—as the ones she wrote home from Taipei during those first two years. She never lost her love of parties and outings, or clothes and décor, all of which were prominently featured in her letters. But she also continued to find remarkable encounters or tragic situations or absurd miscommunications to eagerly describe; Coletta was right about her intense curiosity. So she hadn't given up the habit of correspondence. Only jettisoned those particular correspondents, Rose and Esther and the rest of her former friends back in Washington. Jettisoned those particular friends, and the former persona she must have felt they tied her to. I saved none of the letters she wrote to me—I have hardly saved anything, living out of a backpack, as I have mostly done throughout my life—but now that Lewis has given me the scrapbook and Lily is gone, I wish I had.

I never saved the letters I received from Lily or anybody else, and no one's ever returned any of the few letters that I wrote, either. I have no old datebooks, journals, no crumpled boarding passes, no snapshots. I don't even have my old passports, which would be documentary evidence. So it's hard for me to accurately reconstruct the chronology of where I've gone and what I've done. It's hard for me to know, not what I've missed so much as when I missed it—where I might have been when I was in the wrong place. I'm talking about political developments, historical cataclysms, the grinding tectonic plates and general disintegration of life on the planet. I faced the consequences of some of these things almost daily—genocides, natural disasters, failing states—but at such close range as to obscure my perspective. Like wearing reading glasses on the street: everything more than two feet from your face is a blur. Then, when I worked at the resorts, I never glanced beyond the property boundaries. If I did so it was only metaphorically, to work the crossword in *TimesFax*. And I was never good at puzzles when the clues had to do with current events or popular culture.

Until I moved here, I never really watched TV. When we arrived in Taiwan in 1957, it didn't exist over there, so any television habit I might have been developing from those TV-dinner evenings in Bethesda was interrupted. I suppose they had TV in Hong Kong by the following year, but we didn't have TVs at St. Botolph's. By the time I got to college in Ann Arbor, it just never occurred to me to watch, and that was that. But my condo here in Honolulu came with cable already installed, so I gave it a try. I spent a few evenings, or maybe weeks, clicking through the offerings. I sampled shows that people raved about and insisted I would like, but it doesn't work to watch your first, you know, *Saturday Night Live* at the age of 66 when you've been out of the United States for most of a half-century. It's like trying to make sense of that street opera in Taipei without ever learning a word of Chinese or knowing any of the fables. I found documentaries on TV that were more intelligible, and soothing. Films about coral reefs and African game parks and the British monarchy. And then I came across Ken Burns' *The Vietnam War*. I guess soothing wasn't the only effect I was after. It made me feel connected to that history anew. I watched it through, rapt, and then went on to view feature-film versions of the Vietnam story. *Apocalypse Now, The Deer Hunter, Full Metal Jacket.* The Burns documentary is the one that really caught me, though. I've watched it multiple times, all ten episodes. Doing so is no longer painful to me. It's helped me make some sense of all those years, and to locate myself within them. I sometimes put it on when I'm trying to sleep, the way other people use a white noise machine. That's bizarre, almost embarrassing to admit: the Vietnam War as soporific.

Anyway, about Jordy. I knew how to fill in around Rosemary's sketchy sightings of him in Taipei in '64, '65, '66, after his college career crashed and burned. The two of them hardly moved in the same circles, so it's not as if these path-crossings were frequent. Her father was a minister of state, while Jordy, despite his origins and protectors, despite his smattering of street Chinese, and despite whatever job title Brad may have bestowed on him at CAT, Jordy was at that point—let's face it, although Lily couldn't ever bring herself to do so—a clerk, a dogsbody. Jordy turned 21 then, the age at which State retracted dependents' diplomatic passports, health insurance, and annual first class "educational travel" between the States and their parents' post abroad. He no longer lived in a big house in a walled garden in a precinct of officialdom. Jordy was on his own, making his stumbling way in a world he both knew and couldn't quite handle. For better or worse. I don't have to tell you which.

He did still receive invitations, lobbed in like missiles from our parents' world, his former world. He was sometimes present at the boating parties, for example. Rosemary once described seeing him, reeling drunk, step right off the bow of Brad's cabin cruiser into the Tamsui River, which conventional wisdom held was entirely polluted. She recounted the clamor of fishing him out and rinsing him off. "Too funny," she wrote. "They poured bottles of gin over his head. So cute! I never heard that he got sick at all. Maybe the river is not as dirty as people say. Or a bottle of gin is the thing to always carry in one's purse, just in case." Rosemary still presents a slightly frivolous affect in her occasional letters, even though she became a pediatrician and then a hospital administrator and then Taiwan's first female cabinet member—with the public health portfolio—and is now retired and living with her plutocrat husband in a villa on Grass Mountain. I haven't actually been to Taipei in decades, not since my parents moved on. Although Taiwan came hurtling out of poverty and has been excused from war, it somehow never became a must-see travel destination, despite its dynamism and stunning natural beauty. In other words, it has had no need for either of my job skills, war- or leisure-related. And I had no need for it. Too many memories.

Jordy still went to the boating parties, but the fact is that he always preferred air to water. When he returned to Taipei on his own, he mostly hung out with flyboys from the U.S. Air Force base, crashing for a while, no doubt against regulations, with a couple of junior officers at their billet. And he lived for the stories of the veteran pilots at CAT. At that early point, most of them were still old Flying Tigers, Yanks who'd fought to keep the Communists from taking China. Jordy retold some of their stories in his letters to me, in renditions that emphasized atrocities—of which there were plenty, committed by both the Japanese and the Communists and surely by the Nationalists too, although those last went undescribed by him. At the time, I thought he was just trying to upset me with gory details, the epistolary analogue of a spider down his sister's back.

160

But now I think this is when Jordy's fierceness about Communism had annealed, that fierceness that would have him eventually devote himself to the fight. He loved and felt at home in China, as did all of us Norells—at home in the then-vestigial China of Taiwan, in the frantically industrious little China of Hong Kong, those fragments of China we knew personally. The China we knew had been good to us. It was a vantage point from which the frightening People's Republic appeared as an unimaginably vast death camp, chillingly reminiscent of the situation of Europe's Jews under the Nazis. Like most people back then, we didn't want to know too much about that kind of thing—Holocaust obsession, Holocaust literature, and academic Holocaust studies being phenomena of more recent vintage. Or maybe it was just because we were Americans, and Foreign Service brats, and believers in the promises of the postwar Pax Americana, and had heard first-person stories like Hsiu's, that the slaughterhouse tales of Red China resonated for us in a sickening way. Well, it was. A slaughterhouse, I mean. And sickening.

Surely Lily heard about Jordy from Rocky, and from Coletta. Coletta had been back to the States to graduate school—international relations at Georgetown—and then returned to Taipei as the mission's Assistant Executive Officer. She had correctly sensed that a few exceptional possibilities were about to open up for Black people, even Black women, and that she might have a reasonable career at State beyond being a secretary. She ended up moving through several USAID and embassy postings in Asia, ending her career on the China desk in Foggy Bottom. Along the way, she married another Foreign Service Officer she met when they were both in Manila. I never knew him—there was a long stretch of years when I never saw

Coletta. He was older and left her widowed. After that, she retired to her bungalow in the hills above Berkeley, in which all the things she collected during her years in Asia do look exquisite, and as if they belong.

On the evening of the day in 1966, in Taipei, when Jordy received his notice to report for induction into the service, it was to Coletta that he went. She no longer lived in a diminutive Japanese house, but in one of the big Western-style ones that were reserved for the Foreign Service. The Vietnam War was an inescapable presence by then. A year later, there would be more than half a million American troops in Vietnam. Earlier, when he turned 18, Jordy had registered with the Selective Service office in Bethesda using our home address. Such a high percentage of boys from that affluent locale went to college, virtually all of whom automatically received student deferments, that the pool of potential draftees from which the Bethesda office could meet its quotas was always small. I don't suppose Jordy had calculated the likelihood that he would be among that number when he abandoned college.

When his notice to report for induction came, Jordy considered it an honor being called to duty, as well as an opportunity. Life had handed him lemons and he was determined to make a gin fizz. When he got his induction notice, he went straight to Coletta—eager and proud, she described him—to ask her advice about which service to opt for. Draftees weren't typically given a choice, but Jordy understood that he wasn't a typical draftee. He had connections. And he used them to join the Marines. And in the Marines, he got his wish. He became a helicopter pilot. It was an incredibly useful machine for this new kind of war conducted in jungle and mountains and against an irregular army. And so useful, too, for clandestine operations such as infiltrations and exfiltrations—the dropping off and rescuing of secret agents—or unacknowledged firebombing strikes, in which the ordnance was a version of napalm home-brewed from Tide and gasoline by the pilots themselves in makeshift hangers at airstrips which were not officially acknowledged to exist. But for Jordy, that dark kind of activity came later, after his hitch in the Marines was up and he went to work again for CAT, flying helicopters in Laos and Thailand—countries into which our undeclared war did not officially spill, where Americans engaged in work like his were there but not there, like ghosts. He was flying, I mean, for Air America.

* * *

Esther was irritated because Lily had drifted from her Jewishness, or had outright rejected it. Or was Esther only upset because Lily had abandoned and rejected Esther? It was a bit of both, I suppose. Esther didn't like losing control. But there certainly was a break with religion in our family's history, and it did coincide with moving overseas. Not that we ever discussed it, or made an overt decision, or a collective one. Jordy and I did have some minor Jewish education. We had gone to both Hebrew school and Sunday school—it was a rather assimilationist temple that my parents helped found in Montgomery County. Jordy had his bar mitzvah. Two years earlier, I had been in the confirmation class; bat mitzvahs, for girls, were almost unknown at the time, at least where we came from. Lily describes a few Jewish observances in Taipei. Maybe early on, when she missed her friends so sorely, having the semblance of a Jewish community there gave her some comfort. I think Lily was just nervous, stepping off the plane that first day, eager to blend into a milieu that she knew would be more mainstream, fully aware that the power in that little grouping on the tarmac resided with the very gentile Dyson van Kirk, Sid's boss, and his tightly wound wife. Lily was worried about her manners, perhaps. And Ella's loud eagerness to connect at the tribal level unnerved her, threatening to undermine her self-control, her ability to pass, threatening guilt by association for the infraction of being different.

After those one or two occasions during our first tour in Taipei, I don't think my family ever observed another Jewish holiday or ceremony. For one thing, after the first year, we kids were hardly around. So, to whatever extent it had all been for our benefit—to inculcate the rising generation, as the observance of religious tradition largely is within families—that impetus was gone. And by the time of that first home leave, Lily had found new friends, none of whom was a Jew, though each of them was like a Jew, other in some way: Gladys, Coletta, and Rocky, marked respectively by addiction, ethnicity, and mystery.

It's odd that Lily turned away from Rose and Esther, since they had been such close friends of hers. But Lily wasn't looking back. Not looking back to being Jewish, that's for sure.

Sid died when he was away from Jakarta, off somewhere else in Indonesia inspecting an agricultural installation or a new clinic or more likely plotting with an anti-Communist warlord, or whatever all those trips were for. For him, of course, we did not sit shiva. We wouldn't have even done that at home in Bethesda, in our assimilated milieu. And there was no Jewish funeral—or even a possibility of there being one, since there were virtually no Jews in Jakarta, let alone any synagogues, rabbis, or Jewish cemeteries.

It's not that there was no marking of the event. After she heard that Sid was dead, even before his body had been brought back to the capital, Lily began to move around the house in a distracted, slurred way—Hsiu told me this—like Gladys Walter fixing things up for another madcap party. Lily was concocting a pastiche of Chinese funereal details. Her porcelain head of Kwan Yin and her antique brass buddha and all the various artifacts and pieces of sculpture she had collected over the years, whether significant in some Asian religion or not, she draped in red paper. She ordered six or eight of those enormous funeral wreaths of white flowers, and even had a photo of Sid blown up for the center of the biggest—it must have been a passport photo, in which he was wearing his usual bow tie and nothing-revealed expression. But then, what would you expect of Sid? She had incense and candles burning everywhere, and all the lamps were dimmed. His body however—and this was a departure from Chinese tradition—was not on display, since it had been cremated.

There was no procession or burial, either, as the Chinese would have done. But friends and acquaintances did come to the house to eat and drink, and by the time they arrived—by the time I arrived, anyway—Lily was bright and focused as ever, ironic, urging people to enjoy, reminding them that at a Chinese funeral there would have been gambling and professional mourners in the courtyard. In place of this, she put on cassettes of the jangly, bangy opera music we used to hear in the streets of Taipei. Meanwhile, Hsiu and the houseboy, in white jackets with frog closures at the collar, passed through on silent black cloth slippers bearing trays of cold drinks and little sandwiches. Crustless sandwiches.

This was not quite the circling in of a community of friends that would have taken place in Bethesda. That would have centered over coffee and rugelach and maybe schnapps, a circling of friends of long duration and shared origin. Lily had been in Jakarta then for six years, but I don't believe she had made any enduring friendships there. She knew everybody, Lily always knew everybody, but she had no close friends of long duration at all anymore, aside from Coletta and Rocky. And Hsiu.

Coletta was in Saigon at the time. It was February 1975, those vortex-like mad last weeks of the war. Coletta couldn't get away. Perhaps she was busy planning the evacuation, though it famously transpired in a frenzy that overwhelmed any planning. Jordy, already having been repositioned to Vietnam by Air America, and who was equally entangled in this imminent disaster, managed to get to Jakarta just for a day by hitching rides on flights in and out via Manila. At the time, I was working in Indonesia at one of the boutique resorts that were opening up in Bali. It was a job I had found through Lily—or rather, a job Lily had found for me through one of her many influential acquaintances in the government and business community of the capital.

It was only a distance of about 600 miles from Bali to Jakarta, but I didn't have an easy trip. For some reason I can no longer remember, it wasn't possible for me to fly up to the capital. Had there been a crash that shut down the airport in Bali? That happened often enough back then in that part of the world. Anyway, I took a taxi into Denpasar, a bus from there to the ferry, a train from the ferry to Surabaya and a then second one to Jakarta, a city I hardly knew, where I got off at the wrong station—about 30 hours after I'd set out. I caught an auto-rickshaw, moving through the city's blare and stink and humid grime, to the house. When I finally dragged myself and my bag up to the gate, it was Rocky Perreira—free as always to travel at will—who answered the bell.

* * *

The Little Sea Hut. *Not a bad idea for a hideaway.*

I can hear it now, as if she were speaking it aloud. Jokingly. Suggestively? I picture a slightly lifted eyebrow, a small pregnant smile. She made the comment as if Rose and Esther would know just what she meant. We hadn't been in Taipei more than two months when she wrote that. Hide away from what? And with whom? Had evasion and escape ever been a topic of conversation among those three women before? If so, why was Esther so irked by Lily's relationship—that ambiguous term—with Rocky Perreira? Or was escape an idea that was just occurring to Lily for the first time?

Coletta said, when I visited her another time in Berkeley, "Your mother, like so many in her position, was always at pains to construe things in the best light. Well, we all were. It comes with the territory, that seamless, faultless surface. You quickly learn to construct a pleasant face. So much can be hidden behind it." Coletta passed me a bowl of grapes. It was an incised celadon bowl, very old, delicately crazed, possibly Yuan Dynasty. It had been Lily's, although Lily had never used it. Lily only put it out for display. "As dear to me as she was, as able to draw me out about my private affairs—and Lauren, I treasured

167

her for that—I must concede that I never understood the state of relations between your mother and dad." She plucked a grape. "Did you?" I didn't have an answer.

Lily's other enduring relationship—forged early in Taipei—was with the orphans. The lost or parentless or unwanted of an entire continent might have seemed abstract. But standing in an overcrowded dormitory, the converted living room of a once-grand house now gone shabby, in an institution run by a once-prosperous lady now reduced to begging help, surrounded by mental cases, polio cases, sickly babies, children with scalps and faces covered with horrible sores? It was all too palpable. Still, like the shoeless pedicab drivers and cart pushers and impossibly burdened coolies trudging through Taipei's muddy streets, the orphans did not require her acknowledgement as individuals—certainly not once she had withdrawn to the tranquil enclosure of her garden walls draped green and gold in ever-blooming allamanda—where she could think about them as a phenomenon, a challenge, a project, while sipping her gimlet.

And her empathy, her pain of recognition, was soon enough directed into useful tasks. Chairing committees, organizing benefits, soliciting donations of bulk goods and then sweet-talking generals into arranging their delivery via Uncle Sam's extensive logistical networks: Lily was good at all of this, and was well-placed to do it. It distinguished her and gave her standing. It became her signature, like a chop—China's traditional carved seal of authorship—with which she could impress repeatedly over time, in Saigon, in Bangkok, in Jakarta, and in Hong Kong. Modern Asian history cooperated generously by providing multitudes of forlorn and abandoned children, thanks to poverty, war, despotic regimes, and the

168

consequent shattered families and mass migrations. There was always too much to do.

I don't mean to say that Lily's work lacked sincerity or value. More than once, she and I found ourselves collaborating, such as when they were posted in Bangkok and I was at a relocation center on the Thai-Cambodian border. Lily and I communicated unofficially—our own little back channel, we liked to joke, although it wasn't any secret—to arrange for the transfer of some kids whose village had been napalmed and whose families had been incinerated and whose own bodies were badly burned, to an orphanage there in the capital that had a medical staff—there, in Thailand, where the war was across a border but still hugely present as an engine of local industry and corruption. Once she had retired to Hong Kong, where thousands of Vietnamese boat people were finding themselves in refugee camps in the years following the debacle of 1975, Lily's efforts shifted direction. She was still concerned with children, but now she devoted her energy and her network of contacts in Asia and the U.S. government to reuniting dislocated and shattered families, helping children who might have appeared to be orphaned to find their surviving parents. Or not. It was genuinely important work. She might easily have enjoyed a thoroughly idle retirement. So I respect her for it.

But Lily and her orphans, the orphans of Asia. Jordy and me? Should I count us in that number?

* * *

We were seldom together as a family after Taipei, although we were all still in Asia. It's a big place, and back then it was far less developed, and was war-torn, so harder to travel around in—though I don't suppose that's what kept us apart. Jordy was certainly mobile enough when he was with Air America. The pilots got a week off every month for R and R because they normally worked straight through the other three, being shot at all day long and experiencing various other kinds of danger and unpleasantness. As "airline" employees, they could travel on any other carrier at ridiculously discounted reciprocal fares. Jordy, who was mostly based at a secret airfield in northern Thailand, would fly Cathay Pacific for something like $20 from Bangkok to Hong Kong. And since Air America had offices at the Peninsula, their pilots could stay there for a similarly laughable rate, be picked up at the airport in the hotel Rolls, and have their bags unpacked for them by the hotel butler.

And then what did they do for Rest and Recreation? They shopped. Mikimoto pearls for their girlfriends and wives. Housefuls of custom-made furniture and antiques to be shipped back to Bangkok or Udorn or Vientiane, where their families were living during their AA hitches—those of the flyers, unlike Jordy, who had families. And Italian shoes, tailored clothes, watches. Air America pilots didn't wear uniforms, but they all had huge, glinting, thousand-dollar Rolex President watches—that would be a thousand-circa-1975 dollars; do the math—heavy as artillery pieces on their wrists. When I happened to see any of those guys in airport terminals or hotel lounges, or when they occasionally delivered an AID field officer to inspect a relief operation where I was working, I never actually saw any of them wearing their fine Hong Kong clothes. But you knew them by those watches. They also drank while in Hong Kong. At least, Jordy drank.

I met up with Jordy in Hong Kong one time in the early Seventies. I hadn't seen him for a couple of years, not since he'd finished his hitch in the Marines and changed employers. Jordy had become a good-looking young man. Girls ran after him when he was 18, 22, though none of them seemed to stick. I'd heard a series of reports over the years that he was going steady with someone, which were always followed shortly by news that they'd broken up. That intel stopped coming when he joined the service. Now, closing in on 30, he looked haggard, going to paunch. He still had that habit, or trick, of allowing a half-smile to pass across his face like a wedge of sunlight crossing the landscape when the clouds moved away. As if pleasure, or the humor in a joke, only dawned on him slowly. It could actually make you feel appreciated, if you were the one who'd told the joke. It was like he was really thinking it through and finally deciding it worked, rather than easily letting out a guffaw just because the rhythm of the conversation called for one. Although if you knew him—and I knew him—it felt more like being manipulated.

For the three days we were together on that visit, it seemed as if he did nothing but suck down gin. "Twelve hours bottle to throttle," he recited, that half-smile standing in for a smirk. Twelve hours without booze before flying, that was the rule for pilots at Air America. When they were working, they stayed high on other substances—amphetamines, cocaine no doubt, adrenaline, fear, machismo. Jordy's particular drug of choice was passion for the good fight, the slugfest with Communism. "So gimme a break, Laur. I don't drink in country even when I'm on the ground. Ever heard the other meaning of R and R? Refuel and Refit. That's what I'm here to do." As a matter of fact, in addition to getting tanked, he did visit his tailor for a fitting.

But what else should Jordy have done there? He had long ago seen the sights. He could hardly have taken a whore for those three days anyway, what with me having traveled there at some effort to be with him. He did not have a house to accumulate things for. Neither of us ever had a place of our own, except for this spare condo I bought once I retired. It seems odd when I consider Lily's flair as homemaker and hostess, when I remember how much she always devoted to creating a showplace where she loved to entertain, and when I picture the homes where we passed our childhoods, in Bethesda and—so briefly, but so memorably—in Taipei. Taipei was the last place we all lived together as a family. And really, that was just a split second in the scheme of things. Later, CAT and Air America took Jordy back to Taipei many times, but he didn't put down roots there, either.

Nor did he have a local friend to hang out with in Hong Kong, although he certainly knew people in the city. During that visit, I was staying out at Repulse Bay with Anna Tarbell, a classmate from St. Botolph's; relief workers got no consideration at the Peninsula. Anna was an Anglo-Indian girl with whom I'm still in touch; she had gone to Oxford and then into the Foreign Office and eventually back to Hong Kong in the colonial administration. Maybe teenage boys don't make lasting friendships like that. Or maybe Jordy didn't. He told me, with an air of boasting, about the camaraderie among the guys he flew with, the hijinks and practical jokes when they were off-duty, the unhesitating risks they would take to pluck a downed buddy to safety. But I don't think Jordy had any real friends. Although, as I have said, it is a hard thing to know about someone else, never mind being a hard thing to define.

So memorable, but so brief. Taipei, I mean. Hardly a moment. For me, anyway. Packed off after a year to this other foreign place where my mother loved to visit and had her other reasons to visit apart from us. Another reason. Well, two other reasons, if you count the shopping.

It was a dreary, sedentary encounter, those few days with Jordy in Hong Kong. Finally, moved by vague nostalgia and the gathering claustrophobia of the Peninsula's dark bar at 11 a.m., I managed to drag him out for a ride on the Peak Tram. Since we'd first gone up to the Peak with Lily and Coletta in 1958, a monstrous concrete entertainment mall had been built. It was an immense brutalist tub bizarrely held aloft on giant piers, so top-heavy you felt it might collapse onto you and then go crashing down the mountain, wreaking terrible destruction on the city below. This hardly suited the sentimental mood I was trying to create. I wanted to connect with my brother for once, which is why I had come to Hong Kong, and which is why I insisted we go up there. Next to this architectural monstrosity, the genteel old Peak Café was still in operation. It occupied a 19th Century stone bungalow with a broad terrace where, on that afternoon with Coletta and mom, we had taken a table for tea and scones and crustless sandwiches—unless I am confabulating another memory.

It was drizzling and foggy the day Jordy and I revisited it, so we sat inside. He ordered gin again. By now, I was tired of watching him drink, and ordered one too. We caught glimpses through the mist of the city below, newly bristling with high-rise towers and well on its ascent to the vertigo-inducing

173

domain it has become. One of those towers would become Lily's final hideaway, her Little Sky Hut.

Picking up his drink and resuming his monologue from the tram, from the taxi before that and the hotel bar earlier, Jordy said, "Week or two ago, I had to run this load of dead bodies back to their village. Hmongs? You know, they work for us, fight for our side. Sabotage jobs, recon, they know how to move in the jungle. Fierce little guys when you give them guns. Corpses stacked up in my bird like fucking firewood—I don't know, twenty of them, twenty-five—guess their unit hit a spot of bad luck. Dead a few days and pretty aromatic. Pfffft. I still can't get the fucking smell out of my nostrils. So we put down in the village and it's all kids and wives and grandmothers moaning and wailing. Who wouldn't? Their future piled up stiff on the ground—this fucking war. You get these smells that won't go away. Burning rubber, cordite. Even regular market smells, frying tofu, *nam pla*, durian stink—nothing to do with the war. I smell them even when I'm nowhere near a market. Turns my stomach. Sometimes I really do heave.

"Something's wrong with me, Laur. This fucking war has done something to my olfactory—I ought to see a doc. An ear, nose, and throat man. Is this a condition? I feel like I'll be smelling the stink of it for the rest of my life. Wherever I go. Take R and R down to the beach at Pattaya and I can't smell the ocean cause I've still got burning rubber in my nose, so what's the point? The lobby of the Peninsula here, those masses of flowers? I just get the scent of blood and metal up my nose. Right now, I smell rotting fruit. Why is that, Laur? It makes it very hard for me. Very hard.

"But why are you here, Laur?"

174

Three drinks later, we were on the Star Ferry back to Kowloon. "What about Rocky?" I asked him. "Rocky and mom?" We were leaning out at the railing, even though it was raining. Jordy had insisted. He was nearly insensate by then.

"Rocky? Love the guy," Jordy said. "I wouldn't be flying if it hadn't been for Rocky—well, him and Brad. He got me my first job with CAT, and then one thing led to another. Haven't seen Rocky in a while. When I first came up to Udorn, he was running things in Bangkok and used to show up at the base a lot. Introducing us to the customer and all that."

"Rocky is the customer, don't you think?"

"It's just a manner of speaking, Laur. We're all on the same side."

Were we? Was I on any side? Jordy and I were both consumed by the war but had been drawn into its whirlwind from clearly different—if not diametrically opposite—places. There are always more than two sides, although the weak ones get submerged in the main conflicts. And some people's stances can be hard to discern, which is often enough on purpose. Jordy needed a side. He needed an organized effort to slot into. Though he really seemed to thrive in an effort that was not too tightly organized, an environment where everybody pulled in the same direction, but their quirks could splay out around the edges. As long as the job got done.

I understand now that Jordy had real problems. Diagnosable problems. Depression, maybe. People didn't think back then that depression was a chemical issue. Today, he could have been prescribed anti-depressants and ended up just fine, assuming that somebody had acknowledged his troubles and offered him some treatment, and that he'd have been willing to accept it. Assuming that a chemical imbalance was all that was wrong. But by that point, years into his deep involvement with the war, he also probably had PTSD. And that wasn't even considered a diagnosis yet. If the symptoms were recognized, it was called shell shock. Still, shell shock was understood to define what happened to combatants who were shot at or bombed. Nobody understood that it also affected the ones within their capsule of false airborne safety who were actually dropping the bombs.

I'm not a psychologist. I'm not on this Earth to deconstruct my troubled brother. But I loved him. Or pitied him. I definitely miss him and long to have him here now to unravel the history we share. We shared. I need him if I'm ever going to answer these questions. That need will never be met. And the questions, I suppose, will never be resolved.

Acknowledging troubles was not a prominent feature of Lily and Sid's parenting style, what with Lily being more concerned with style and what we now call "lifestyle," and Sid being concerned with whatever Sid was concerned with—Sid having been, without a doubt, the customer, too. A tough customer: aloof, masked and impenetrable, as you might expect a spy to be. Unlike Rocky, whose ebullience somehow worked as both banner and shroud for his clandestine activities. Anyway, without support, and lacking therapy or prescription, Jordy found a cause and an outfit to join so as to make up for his inability to navigate on his own. Of course, you could say I did the same thing. My cause was fueled by war too. It allowed me to remain a nomad just as much as Jordy's did, not committed to any individual persons. But it did allow me to hang on to Asia.

Always near, but not with, my family.

Like a career diplomat, I possessed only a notional home—Bethesda, and the split-level contemporary where we lived as kids, but which I had not set eyes on since 1957. Neither Jordy nor I ever built a conventional adult life, if there is such a thing in this world. You could say Jordy didn't live long enough to do so, but it did not seem to be in the cards for him, anyway. As for me, it's only since I retired that I actually possess more than a single towel, or that I've furnished a kitchen with cookware and gadgets. Because of what I came from, even decades after I was no longer a Foreign Service dependent, I could move between the worlds of Asia—where there are so many worlds. The world of evacuees and the world of vacationers. Anna Tarbell's house in Repulse Bay, where I used to stay in Hong Kong before Lily settled there, and the hot springs lodge at Sun Moon Lake, where I took Serge in '77 to recuperate. I still traveled as fluidly as if I held a U.S. diplomatic passport even when I no longer did.

I correct myself: I did make that one return visit to Taiwan, to Sun Moon Lake, with Serge. Serge was a doctor from Marseilles whom I first met in Bangladesh when we both joined the emergency response to that terrible cyclone in 1970. If I never made a home, I did make a few connections over the years. He was not the only lover, but was the only one who ever mattered, and was also the one who got away. After Bangladesh, Serge and I crossed paths and worked together repeatedly, sometimes accidentally and to our dismay, but sometimes on purpose because we kept wanting to try again, until we finally stopped. After Cambodia fell to the Khmer Rouge in '75,

Médecins sans Frontières set up its first refugee mission in Thailand. In '76, he asked me to join him there. Sid and Jordy had both died during the previous year. I was ready to leave Bali and the luxurious boredom of hospitality work and get back into the dirt, into work that wouldn't leave me any energy or space for brooding. And I was hopeful about getting back with Serge, at the time.

That was the hardest place of all to do our kind of work. The Cambodians trickling over the border to us were the most traumatized people I'd seen. What they were escaping was not only unutterably brutal but bizarre enough to stupefy even thick-skinned relief veterans like us who thought we had seen it all. I said I took Serge to Sun Moon Lake to recuperate—he'd gotten malaria—but after a year of dealing with refugees from those Cambodian killing fields, we both needed R and R. Naturally, Lily knew somebody to call. Several somebodies, in fact. Rocky, for one, who arranged to comp our flights on CAT, and then whoever lent us that bungalow for a month. I forget who that was, some Taipei plutocrat or government minister...yes, it was an official government guest house, now that I recall. On the way there, we had a long afternoon to kill in Hong Kong before our connecting flight. Lily had just set up house with Hsiu in Mid-Levels and she had us over to lunch. It was the only time she met Serge, but she approved in a big way. He was, after all, both a doctor and French. Lily was still a Francophile, and still a Jewish mother. Hsiu liked him, too. Or liked the fact that he was in my life.

At the lake, we slept and sat on the verandah watching the mist rise. We took sulfur baths and had massages, and when our minds were cleared and our tremors were calmed, when we felt a little stronger, we made love. There was a little sailboat we went out in, and on the placid water of that mountain lake I remembered how to use it. It was peaceful there, not just because of the remoteness and natural beauty, but because war was distant enough to seem unreal. Taiwan hadn't seen any military conflict since the days when that ridiculous bomb shelter had been installed in our garden two decades earlier. And it still hasn't to this day. I hoped that in such a cool, cloud-forest interlude, Serge and I might—but never mind, we didn't. I haven't seen him for years and years now. I understand that he married, settled down back in France, specialized in infectious diseases and was involved in the important early research on AIDS. That was in the '80s, the last of him I've ever heard. Old news long since. I've never sailed again, either.

"But Rocky and mom?" I asked Jordy again.

Jordy stopped and let me catch up. I had just followed him back into the hushed, polished lobby of the Peninsula. He turned to face me. For the first time on that visit, and perhaps for the first time in years, he seemed clear, oddly at peace. He spoke quietly. "Why even ask? She'll never tell. And he'll never tell the truth."

* * *

Serge was my last lover, if lover means someone with whom you are in love. That was such a long time ago. On the other hand, if lover means someone you have sex with once, or a shallow affair that lasts a bit longer, then I should say that there have been others. Not with any of the frequency and ziplessness of the zipless fuck, circa 1970—free love turned out to have its costly consequences. Anyway, when you're older, the body isn't so perpetually on call; nor does it so insistently do the calling. Not mine, at least. But still.

About five years after I last saw Serge, I was in one of my concierge phases, working at a place on the Queensland coast. It was one of those that ferried guests out to dive the reef every day by helicopter. I had come to detest the whomp-whomp of those machines after Jordy died. I never climbed into one again, either. But I wasn't obliged to; my job was to keep the guests content, not to swim with the fishes. A letter came one day from Lily in Hong Kong: Rocky would be in Sydney, he would love to see me, why don't I take a break and go down there? I hadn't seen Rocky since that time in Jakarta, right after Sid died. I hadn't been off the property for a couple of months, and I was bored. Besides, it was the slow season.

I met Rocky at the hotel where he was staying, a tower with a rooftop lounge overlooking the bay. We met in the late afternoon for cocktails. Rocky was maybe 62 then, I around 40. He seemed restrained, contained, in contrast to the old bonhomie. There was something inward and reflective about his energy. It made him mysterious in a different way, although just as alluring. Rocky was one of those handsome men who only gets better looking as they age. His hair was still thick and black, but was threaded with silver, his face had not collapsed but looked thinner and sculpted. His ready grins had given way to angular little smiles. Wistful smiles.

We talked about a lot of things, but he mostly wanted to talk about Jordy. He felt responsible. "I helped him get where he wanted to go, and then in the end, I didn't really pay attention," Rocky said. "I didn't bother to realize. It galls me, Lauren—you know, I saw him pretty often during that last year of the war, but it was always just a quick 'Hey, man, everything good?' You know, our guys in the war, you knew some of them, how they talked, the pressure they were under. I didn't try to find out how he *was*, and of course we all knew we were losing that fight. It was going down fast. Although, you didn't talk about that. You only brought it up with people you felt close with—but, I mean, I'd known Jordy since he was a kid, so why wasn't he someone I would—your brother—" His voice caught, or maybe it was a hiccup. "Well, I knew him as a boy."

It seemed he might weep. He turned away, to gaze in the fading light at that billion-dollar view: the soaring white shells of the Opera House, streams of headlights and taillights flowing red and white through the dusk as they crossed the Harbour Bridge, ferries gliding to and from Circular Quai. The whole panorama in motion was utterly silent from where we watched. I thought, this wistfulness—it's because he's seeing me again. After all this time, after everything. And I thought not of Jordy but of Serge, Serge's slender hands in blood-spattered latex gloves—that war, I knew something about it, too.

The elevator lobby had glass walls, and while we waited there, Rocky reached out. Toward me. I reached toward him and took his hand in mine. I'd had an older man or two, but none like this one, so beautiful, so familiar, known but unknown. For a moment, I couldn't think straight. But then I had two thoughts in one instant:

I want him.

And,

I will betray my mother.

Rocky lightly accepted my hand, and then, understanding, quickly shrugged toward the view, a gesture that urged us both to turn in that direction, and caused our two hands to part. "Oh," he said quietly. "Oh, no, Lauren." He had understood my thoughts. I suppose he had been in situations like this so many times before, a man like Rocky. He said, "I mean, my dear girl, I just wanted to show you something fantastic." He pointed. "There she is." Gleaming in the twilight was a stately ship, big but delicate in form. It was passing behind Bennelong Point where the arcs of the Opera House reprised the sharp curve of its prow. "That's the *QE II* coming into port on her world cruise. Isn't she a beauty? This is a moment we'll never forget."

* * *

The last time I saw Jordy was in August of '75, in Jakarta, at Lily's. He'd washed up there once he was done with Air America, soon after the fall of Saigon that May. Sid had been dead for a few months. With her long and industrious career as a Foreign Service wife thus abruptly terminated, Lily had been procrastinating. She had taken over from State paying rent on the house they'd been living in. Now its lease was coming to an end, while the last of a long line of tenants were about to vacate our family's place in Bethesda. After parking Jordy out from underfoot on the shadowy terrace, Lily finally got busy packing up to go home. I came up from Bali to give her a hand with that. And with him.

Jordy was a mess. Inert, self-medicating, morose but spasmodically vocal. When he talked, it was all about the crashing end of the war, the disastrous retreat from Saigon that he'd been involved in—been consumed by. Lily had fixated on one tiny piece of the debacle, the Operation Babylift catastrophe when a C5-A carrying 300 orphans to asylum in the States crashed in a swamp just after take-off from Tan Son Nhut. Choppers from Air America had helped in the rescue effort, though not Jordy's. His was in for repair that day, so he was at the airbase when they started ferrying the children back. "You couldn't tell them apart," he said in an affectless drone. "Whether they were alive or not. They were all muddy, all bloody. I carried some of them—hardly weighed a thing. The nurses were passing them under a shower and saying, 'Dead. Dead. This one's alive. Dead. Alive.' There was nothing for me to do."

"Oh honey, you did what you could," Lily disagreed. "You helped. That must have been so terrible to see. But some of them were alive!" She was doing a good job of ignoring Jordy's situation. From time to time, she would step out to where he sat on the terrace—a gin clutched squarely in both hands on his lap, bare feet aligned on the tiles—to offer him objects that she was undecided about keeping. Bronze flatware with rosewood handles, a complete service for 16 that she'd picked up in Bangkok. An early Qing Dynasty altar table with delicate fretwork, from the Mainland via Taipei—a lovely piece I wish I'd thought of keeping for myself, now that I have somewhere to put it. She carried on with this while Jordy, who had nowhere to go and nothing to do, wordlessly turned it all down. "Those darling babies," Lily would murmur again. And then, briskly,

"You just need some time, honey. That was hard on you. Get you back flying for somebody, you'll be fine."

Lily and I sorted and wrapped and packed. Hsiu stayed out of it, except for occasionally directing the houseboy to shift a box. He served our meals with a long face, hardly speaking. When I arrived, he had greeted me silently—which was unusual—but with an unusually fierce hug. I guess he was already in mourning for the life he'd had with my parents, and was distressed about Jordy, too. He made sure Jordy always had a glass of icewater on the table at his side, but he refused to pour the gin. One morning, he announced that the houseboy had been dismissed. "Why need houseboy, all you leave here soon? I carry Missy Lily's boxes now. Maybe Jordy can help."

* * *

Lily had gone to bed. The lights were off in the servants' wing. Jordy was still sitting out there in the heavy darkness. I brought out a glass for myself and a bottle of gin stuck into an ice bucket that glistened with beads of sweat. Unbidden, Jordy said, "It was crazy, Laur, those last few days. Everybody in the city was trying to get somewhere else. Like everybody had their own idea of how to save themselves. The streets—you couldn't move. The exchange rate was wild, Americans were buying up everything they could carry away—gold, jewelry—for nothing. For nothing. These people's lives, their life savings, gone for nothing. You knew it was all breaking apart, but you couldn't just leave after putting so much into it. Everything was moving in every direction—just crazy.

184

"Then we started those rooftop landings at the embassy, at USAID—certain apartment buildings—supposed to ferry people to the airport. Americans and some Vietnamese who worked with us or, I don't know, who'd paid somebody to get them on a list. Crowds of other people trying to break into the compounds, marines forcing them back with guns at the gates, on the stairs. Crazy—and ARVN soldiers, the friendlies, when they realized we weren't going to get them all out, they started looting, shooting into crowds for nothing, shooting at us. Hysterical. I saw them drag a girl into an alley and...who knows—I saw that, from the chopper. I saw that. Abandoned them. We abandoned them after all those years. I didn't put my life into that war, get shot at every other time I took off, shit my guts out with dysentery, I didn't live through that hell to abandon them.

"We were supposed to ferry people from those rooftops out to Tan Son Nhut so they could get onto planes for Manila or Brunei or wherever. But the base was just total chaos—crashed planes burning in the runways, and the people mobbing anything that tried to land. ARVN officers pulling guns, trying to commandeer our aircraft. Mothers tossing babies right over people's heads into airplanes. I saw a guy beat his hands bloody on the windows of a plane after they shut the door on him. People climbing onto the wings and landing gear as if they could get away like that, survive. People lost their minds. Lost their minds. Fuck, I had people hanging from my own skids, dropping off my own skids onto the concrete from 100 feet, 200 feet. I saw that looking down. I'm taking off and people are shooting at me, like that's going save anybody's ass. Just lost their fucking minds. They knew what was coming, the ones who had worked with us, the ones in the South Vietnamese

185

government, the ARVN. Nothing to lose by then and they knew it, so they just went insane. Is that why people go insane? Nothing left to lose?"

Jordy paused and I became aware of Lily, not in bed after all, but standing in the open French door. She was weeping. "Those babies," she gasped. "Those beautiful babies." The sounds of night in Jakarta filled the garden. Cars on the street outside the gate. Horns in the distance. Air conditioning compressors. The rattle of palm fronds. A gecko scuttling up the wall. Our mother's quiet sobs. Then Jordy spoke once more. He had to tell this story. I believe he had never told it before.

"We were running low on fuel. We were supposed to refuel at the base, but you couldn't get close to it, you couldn't contact any ground crew, so we started flying out to the fleet instead, putting people down on the ships, fueling up and then back to Saigon for another run. About 45 minutes each way. You didn't know when you headed back in what hell you would find I don't know how many runs I made that last day. Six? Way overloaded, people so crammed in they could hardly breathe. And then it was over.

It was over. And these Navy skippers were ordering our aircraft tossed overboard. Overboard! They just threw our fucking aircraft into the ocean. Why? You're asking me why? You know why. Because we were Air America and we weren't supposed to exist. Like we hadn't been risking our own asses all those years for something we believed in, too. Like we were just some kind of mercenaries. They didn't want any evidence that we'd even been part of it. Like we were some kind of taint on their ships, on them. Which, by the way, *they* lost the fucking war. And then after they threw our choppers into the sea, they practically treated us like a bunch of criminals. Like we had a bad smell. Held a bunch of us AA guys in their officers' mess *with armed guards so we couldn't leave the room.* I thought, for this? It was all for this?"

* * *

That was the last time I saw Jordy. Alive, I mean. I had to go up to Jakarta to identify his body after he died because Lily had returned to Washington already, just the week before. The embassy contacted her, and she told them to reach me at the resort in Bali. Hsiu was still in Jakarta, packing the last of her things to be shipped home. And he, the utterly reliable majordomo, was in a state of total meltdown. I had to take care of him as well as sort out the details of my brother's death. I chose a green stone urn for Jordy's ashes, and had it shipped to Lily. I looked for it later, after her death, in the Hong Kong apartment. But I never saw it again. Maybe she wasn't able to bear keeping it around. Maybe Hsiu had appropriated it and kept it like a treasure in his room, which had previously been her room—once he became the owner of the apartment, the servant's room off the kitchen, his former room, was occupied by a new houseboy, or whatever kind of help he was to Hsiu. A willowy young man recently arrived from someplace in the Chinese interior who could no doubt tell his own tale of escape.

When I got to the morgue in Jakarta, I was given the choice of having Jordy's body autopsied. Why even ask?

I mean it. Because a lot of questions can have several different answers. Such as, why do I sometimes now light the candles on Friday night like a practicing Jew? It might be belief. Perhaps it's just loneliness and nostalgia for family—or for my mother, whom I can recall chanting the blessing at the dining room table in Bethesda while the two little flickers were mirrored in the sliding glass doors. And can there be a single reason why I chose to end up here, to spend my retirement years in a studio apartment in a Honolulu high-rise? Maybe I like the anonymity of this big building and have only a modest need for space. Or maybe because this is an island in the tropics, and a bustling city, the most Asian one in the U.S., and so deeply reminiscent of the other places I've known—but without the entanglements of actually knowing any people here.

Then again, it might be because this is the place from where we flew off for our two years in the Far East, two years that stretched out to determine the course of our four lives. Or because from here, I can picture other places and directions in which our lives might have unfolded. Or perhaps it's because, from my little balcony here, I have a westward view with a glimpse of the ocean, and I can lean out over the railing and pretend I'm seeing all the way—all the way to Taiwan. To Indonesia. To Hong Kong, where Hsiu sits on the balcony that once belonged to Lily. To Vietnam.

It's really not true that I don't know anybody here. There's a Vietnamese woman I'd first met while she and her children were refugees. I helped them get to the U.S., and they settled here in Honolulu. She tracked me down years later to thank me. I have been introduced to other people in the Vietnamese immigrant community through her. I am invited to family feasts during Tet, and when there are weddings, I always wear the jade bracelet Coletta gave me, the twin of one that was Lily's. I can't say that any of these people are close friends. But seeing these families thrive reminds me that I have done something that was worth doing. Even though I have nothing to show for it, and my life is solitary and austere. In this intangible way, I am rich. And at peace.

There is also an elderly couple about my age from Taiwan living in this building. I don't know them well, either, but they were pleased to learn that I once lived in Taipei. We chat in the lobby and at the pool. We make a show of greeting each other in Mandarin, though I have lost whatever proficiency with the language I once had. They are both quite fluent in English and were telling me the other day about a festival they attended when they made a trip home recently to meet their newest grandchild, or great-grandchild. It takes place every third year. The ceremonial burning of a boat at midnight following days of celebration.

Though it's an age-old tradition, I had never heard of this event before, or of the seaside town in the south of the island where it is held. I know Taiwan is prosperous now, efficient and clean, futuristic. But I picture this boat-burning as it surely would have been six decades ago, when I might have conceivably attended: dust from unpaved streets swirling upward with the smoke, fragrances and stinks wafting from the food carts and benjo ditches, the pressing throng, the barefoot kids, the sticky air. I picture my mother moving through the throng in a crisp pale blue shirtwaist, serenely, unaffected by the wilting heat, alert, a bright and genuinely interested expression on her face—with Rocky just a half-step behind. A ritual boat burning is just the kind of thing, both fabulous and arcane, that Rocky would have insisted on dragging us all off to see. I imagine him getting up an impromptu party, or anyway a party that appears to be impromptu. Brad Mencken would be along, mixing cocktails—plus Coletta, Rosemary Ling, Gladys, and Billy from next door. I see Rocky commandeering a shaky, unpressurized CAT C-47 in which he will fly us all down-island from Taipei, with Jordy, still an eager teenager, beaming at everyone from the co-pilot's seat. That would have been fun. Fun should have been Rocky's middle name.

Taipei, Taiwan. Ilha Formosa. And a gorgeous life. From my little balcony here in Honolulu, I notice a plane climb away from the airport in that direction, and I imagine flying across the Pacific one more time, myself. In a throbbing DC-6. In a humming 707. In the lavish Golden Dragon with its elaborate Chinese meals presented on red lacquer trays. Or perhaps in a gorgeous new 787 Dreamliner. The airliner of tomorrow. It's here now.

also by Jonathan Lerner

Caught in a Still Place
Alex Underground
Swords in the Hands of Children

[acknowledgments]

For 15 or 20 years, I had been pondering how to use a collection of vivid letters my mother wrote from Taipei. Then one day, in the supermarket check-out line, I ran into the novelist and literary provocateur Dave King. He asked, "When are you going to give us another novel?" Sometimes all it takes to get moving is a pointed inquiry from a friend. Thanks, Dave.

My family did go to Taipei in 1957. My mother's letters brought the place alive again for me, and Lily's letters borrow some her observations and wit. But Lily is not my mother. Her family and its saga are very much their own.

I completed work on this book during a residency at the Brush Creek Arts Foundation, in Saratoga, Wyoming, for which I am deeply grateful.

About the Author

Jonathan Lerner, born in 1948, grew up in Washington, D.C., with the exception of two years in the late fifties when his father, a Foreign Service officer, was posted to Taipei. That experience, and the journeys there and back which took his family literally around the world, primed a lifelong addiction to travel. It was also the germ for his new novel LILY NARCISSUS.

Lerner matriculated at Antioch College in 1965, but dropped out two years later and immersed himself in New Left activism, joining the staff of Students for a Democratic Society. His early writing experiences were producing SDS publications and contributing to other counterculture and "underground" newspapers. In 1969 he helped found the breakaway SDS faction the Weatherman. That became the clandestine and cult-like Weather Underground, which carried out a campaign of bombings. These experiences—and the challenges of being a young man struggling with his gay identity in a macho group culture—informed both Lerner's novel ALEX UNDERGROUND and his memoir SWORDS IN THE HANDS OF CHILDREN.

"When I stopped trying to be a full-time revolutionary, in the mid-seventies, I embraced my calling to be a full-time writer," Lerner says. His first novel, CAUGHT IN A STILL PLACE, was published in 1989. Meanwhile he had begun establishing what became a successful career as a magazine writer and editor. Early on he wrote mostly travel stories, typically with a design angle. Later he concentrated on topics including architecture, urban planning, and issues of natural resources and sustainability. His work has appeared in The New York Times, Metropolis, The Architect's Newspaper and numerous other publications. He has been a contributing editor at Landscape Architecture Magazine for the last decade.

During the eighties Lerner lived in various parts of Florida, and after that for 21 years in Atlanta. In 2011 he moved to New York's Hudson Valley, to live with Peter Frank, a community advocate, whom he married in 2015.

About the Press

Unsolicited Press was founded in 2012 and is based in Portland, Oregon. The press produces stellar fiction, nonfiction, and poetry from award-winning writers. Authors include John W. Bateman, T.K. Lee, Rosalia Scalia, and Brook Bhagat.

Find the press on Twitter and Instagram: @unsolicitedp